The Hasty Marriage

by

BETTY NEELS

P9-CAN-382

Harlequin Books

TORONTO • LONDON • NEW YORK • AMSTERDAM • SYDNEY

Original hardcover edition published in 1977
by Mills & Boon Limited

ISBN 0-373-02110-0

Harlequin edition published October 1977

Printed in U.S.A.

CHAPTER ONE

LAURA heard the car draw up outside the house while she was still in the kitchen cutting bread and butter for tea, but she didn't stop what she was doing. Her father and Joyce would be in the sitting room waiting for their visitors, and there would be a small delay while they were greeted and ushered indoors; she would be able to slip in at the last minute.

She started to arrange the slices on a plate, reflecting that it would be pleasant to see her godfather again; he had always come to England at least twice a year, but now, since his illness, he lived semi-retired from his medical practice and no longer drove a car. It was fortunate that there had been this old friend who had been coming to England anyway and had suggested that they might travel together. She laid the last slice in its place, washed her hands and went from the nice old-fashioned kitchen, down the back hall and into the sitting room. Old Doctor van Doorn de Pette was there, sitting in one of the large, rather shabby armchairs by the window, talking to her father, and she went straight to him and gave him an affectionate hug.

'Lovely to see you, Godfather,' she exclaimed in her pretty voice. 'You must be tired—tea's all ready.'

He studied her, smiling. 'Dear Laura—not changed, and glad I am of it. Tea will be delightful, but first you must meet my friend, Reilof van Meerum.'

She had been aware of him, of course, talking to Joyce at the other end of the long, low-ceilinged room, but she hadn't looked at him. And now, crossing the polished floor to shake his hand, she hardly heard her godfather saying: 'My goddaughter, Reilof—Laura,' for she was fighting bewilderment and delight and surprise all rolled into one, because at last here was the man she had been waiting for—standing in front of her, all six feet three inches of him, rather heavily built and no longer young—but then she was twenty-nine herself, wasn't she?—and so incredibly good-looking, with his dark hair silvered at the temples and dark eyes under heavy brows. With the greatest effort in the world she composed her ordinary features into a conventional smile of greeting, said 'How do you do?' with a calm she didn't feel and made some remark about his journey. He answered her politely, and when Joyce chimed in, turned back to her with every sign of interest—and not to be wondered at, conceded Laura, as she went back to her father to tell him that she would be bringing in the tea tray in a few minutes, Joyce was worth anyone's interest; pretty —very pretty and fair, with large baby blue eyes, and nine years her junior to boot.

She thought it without envy; from the moment that Joyce had been born, she had been the focal point of the household, and later, of their circle of friends, and although she had been spoilt by her parents, very few had ever discovered the fact. As for Laura, she had quickly come to take it for granted, for when her sister was born she had been a disappointingly gawky child of nine, with light brown hair, straight and fine and worn, for convenience's sake, in two pigtails, and her small face, its childish chubbiness lost, was already settling into its unexciting mould. Only her hazel eyes were fine, large and richly lashed, but even they stood no chance against Joyce's gorgeous blue ones.

It was natural enough that her mother and father should have been delighted to have such a pretty little girl, and she herself had been overjoyed to have a small sister; Laura had spoilt her too, and after their mother had died she had done her best to take her place, but somehow, by the time Joyce was twelve years old, she was already making it plain that she no longer needed Laura for a companion, and it had been a relief to them both when Laura went away to London to train as a nurse. Now, although she came home fairly frequently, she had grown used to Joyce's casual treatment and her assumption that when Laura was home she would take over the burden of the household so that Joyce might be free to go where and when she wanted.

She went back to the kitchen and picked up the loaded tray, and was faintly surprised when Doctor van Meerum crossed the room to take it from her, and caught Joyce's quick frown as he did so—so silly of her to be annoyed, thought Laura, when he was only being polite; surely his quick, impersonal smile made that clear.

The conversation became general during tea, but that didn't disguise the fact that Joyce had captivated their visitor, and indeed she was behaving charmingly. Laura, watching her, thought how nice it must be to attract people—men, she amended honestly—without any effort at all. She took very little part in the talk, but occupied herself with filling the tea-cups and passing plates of cake and sandwiches, replying to any remarks made to her in her unassuming way, and when tea was finished, sitting quietly beside her godfather, listening to him discussing the finer points of an article he had just had published.

While she listened she glanced from time to time at Joyce and Doctor van Meerum, sitting a little apart, deep in a talk of their own. They made a striking pair; Joyce, her cheeks faintly pink with excitement, her eyes wide, had the big, rather silent man beside her already ensnared. Laura told herself that if they were mutually attracted, there was nothing to do about it; he might be the man she had dreamed about for so long, but that didn't mean that she could expect him to fall for her; in any case, while Joyce was around that was so unlikely as to be laughable.

She started to put the tea things back on the tray very quietly, so as not to disturb the conversation, wondering if it might not have been better never to have met Reilof van Meerum than to have found him now only to see him bowled over by Joyce's lovely little face. She went into the kitchen again and washed up, fed Mittens the cat and started to get the supper ready. Presumably the doctor would stay, and anyway one more would make no difference. She put the soup she had made that morning on to heat, for the April evening was chilly, and started on a cheese soufflé. She had made a trifle that afternoon and there was plenty of cheese, and now she poked round in the old-fashioned larder for ingredients with which to make a salad; apples and a tomato or two, a lettuce and a providential head of celery—she mixed a dressing for it, put the soufflé into the oven and went to lay the table.

The dining room looked cosy, for she had had the forethought to light a small fire there; its rather shabby old-fashioned furniture looked pleasant in the light of the shaded lamp over the big mahogany table, the silver shone in it too, and when she had finished she looked at it with satisfaction and then ran upstairs to her room to tidy herself before putting out the drinks. Her room was at the back of the house, square and airy and furnished with the white-painted furniture of her childhood. She sat down before her dressing-table glass, making no attempt to do her face or hair, but staring at her reflection with a critical eye. She wasn't exactly plain, but she wasn't pretty either. Her mouse-brown hair was fine and silky and very long, but as she usually wore it piled on top of her head, its beauty was scarcely seen, and although her eyes were nice they weren't in the least spectacular. Her nose and mouth were just ordinary, and although her figure was pretty she was barely of middle height, and as she tended to dress in an unassuming manner it was seldom that anyone took a second glance at her.

But her mouselike appearance was deceptive; she was a clever girl and a splendid nurse, holding a Ward Sister's post at St Anne's hospital in London, highly prized by the people she worked with and for. Besides, she was a good housewife and cook, got on well with animals and children and was liked by everyone. But she also had a fine temper when roused to anger, which wasn't often, and could be, on occasion, extremely pig-headed. She had long ago come to terms with herself and accepted life as it came, and if it wasn't quite what she had hoped it would be, no one heard her say so. She spoke to her reflection now:

'It's a good thing that you're going back to St Anne's in the morning, my girl, before you start getting silly ideas into your head—out of sight, out of mind, and don't you forget it.' She nodded sternly at herself, smoothed her hair, powdered her un-distinguished nose and went back downstairs, where she was greeted with the news that Doctor van Meerum had accepted Joyce's invitation to stay the night and go on to London in the morning. It vexed her very much to hear her sister declare: 'You can give Laura a lift,' with the certainty of one accustomed to having her every wish granted; she wasn't in the least deceived by his polite agreement to do this—he wanted to please Joyce ...

Laura had plenty of opportunity to observe Doctor van Meerum during supper. His manners were nice and he had undoubted charm; he maintained a steady flow of small talk without monopolising the conversation, said very little about himself, gave his full attention to any remarks addressed to him and showed a sense of humour which delighted her. All the same he was unable to prevent his dark eyes dwelling upon Joyce whenever the opportunity occurred, and his smile, when their eyes met, would have set any girl's heart beating faster. It annoyed Laura that she had no control over that organ and was forced to suffer its thumping and jumping. It almost stopped altogether when they had finished their meal at last and she began to clear the table as the company dispersed to the sitting room, for he turned round at the door to look at her and then walked back into the room, saying, 'You must let me help you ...'

She had no chance to say yes or no, for Joyce had turned round too and cried with careless affection, 'Darling, I'll wash up, you've had all the chores to do—Reilof will help me.' She turned a laughing face to his. 'You will, won't you? although I don't think you do it at home.'

He laughed with her. 'No, I can't say I do, but I see no reason why I shouldn't try my hand at it.' He added, with a quick kindly glance at Laura: 'You must be wanting a chance to talk to your god-father.'

She pinned a cheerful, pleased expression on to her features and agreed untruthfully that there was nothing she wanted more, and slipped away to run upstairs and make up the bed in one of the spare rooms.

The house, although not large, rambled a good deal, with several rather poky passages, unnecessary steps and a variety of windows. The room she went into had a square bay overlooking the flat Essex countryside, flooded in moonlight, and she stood for a minute or two to admire it before she pulled the curtains and began to make the bed. That done, and the room ready for their unexpected guest, she went along to her own room once more to pack her over-night bag; she had had a long weekend and it was a pity that her godfather had arrived only a few hours before she would have to leave. Still, she would be able to come home again at the end of the week, she had Friday evening and a free day on Saturday and it was only thirty or so miles from London. Perhaps Joyce would be free to drive in to Chelmsford and meet her train; if not she could always get old Bates, who ran a taxi service in Rodwell, to fetch her.

She went downstairs again and found the two older gentlemen happily deep in medical matters and no sign of the other two. She fetched the petit-point she was stitching and settled down at a small work table, a lamp at her shoulder, and began to work on it. It was almost two hours later when Joyce and the doctor came in and her sister explained, 'It was such a heavenly moonlit evening, we went for a walk—I hope you didn't miss us?'

Her father paused momentarily to look at her fondly. 'I can't say that we have, my dear, and Laura has been so engrossed in that embroidery of hers that I don't suppose she has either.'

Laura looked up and smiled in the general direction of everyone. 'Such a nice peaceful occupation,' she murmured.

'Oh, Laura,' Joyce laughed, 'you sound just like an old maid, and you're not—at least, not just yet.'

There was general laughter at her joke and Laura joined in, although it wasn't a joke really—Doctor van Meerum would know, if he hadn't realised it already, that she was getting a little long in the tooth. But it wasn't that which hurt, it was knowing that her sister considered her past the age to attract a man's interest and found it amusing.

They set out after breakfast the following morning, she and Doctor van Meerum, in his Aston Martin, and although she had spent a more or less sleepless night, she perked up at the sight of the elegant car—she hadn't seen it the previous evening and she had imagined that he would drive something far more staid; he hadn't struck her as being the type of man to like fast cars.

She couldn't have been more mistaken; he was a superb driver, fast and careful and relaxed. She sat back and enjoyed it all, keeping quiet because she sensed that he didn't want to talk much. They were halfway there and hadn't exchanged more than a few words when he asked suddenly: 'Joyce—she tells me that she has just left her job. Does she intend to become a nurse too?'

Joyce had left several jobs if the truth were to be told; she became bored easily, or the office was too small, the people she worked with not to her liking or she wasn't paid enough ... But Laura was a loyal sister.

'No, I don't think so,' she told him carefully, 'it upsets her to see people who are ill—she's young and it's difficult to decide what one wants to do sometimes. I expect she'll stay at home ...'

'You didn't, you decided,' he persisted.

'Yes, but nursing was something I wanted to do.' She didn't tell him that she had wanted to be a doctor, but somehow it had all fallen through because Joyce had to be educated at the best schools. It had taken her a long time to get over the disappointment. But that had been ten years ago and in that time she had become content enough, but always cherishing the hope that she would meet the man she would want to marry and who would want to marry her—and now she had, and a lot of good it had done her. She roused herself from her thoughts to hear her companion say, 'Joyce is a very lovely girl, she must have any number of men friends.'

'Oh, rather, but not one special one.'

'And you?' he asked, to surprise her.

She told him no rather shortly and briskly

changed the conversation. 'Are you going to be in England long?'

They were driving more slowly now, with London's outskirts creeping upon them from all sides. 'A week or so—I have to go to Birmingham in a few days and then to Edinburgh. I hope I may have the opportunity of seeing you again before I go back.'

'But you'll be driving Godfather home, won't you?'

'Certainly.'

'Oh, you mean to come and see us before then,' she stated forthrightly. 'I'm sure Father and Joyce will love to see you—don't wait to be invited ...'

'Joyce has asked me to stay the night on my way to Birmingham if I could arrange it—perhaps I could give you a lift home? Let me see, it would be on a Friday or Saturday—next weekend.'

'What a pity,' said Laura instantly, longing to accept and perversely determined to do no such thing, 'I've already promised my staff nurse the weekend and I couldn't possibly disappoint her, but thank you for asking.' She would have to remember to give Pat Emery, her right hand on the ward, a long weekend and invent some excuse for not taking her own usual weekend. 'If you would drop me off somewhere along Stratford Broadway, I can pick up a bus. I've heaps of time.'

'I'm going to St Anne's—I have to meet Mr Burnett there.'

She would be seeing Mr Burnett herself in a few hours' time; he was the senior consulting surgeon on Men's Surgical. She said: 'Oh,' rather blankly and added, 'Do you know the way?'

'Yes, thanks.' He demonstrated his knowledge by taking a short cut through the rather dingy streets around them. 'Do you go to Holland to visit your godfather?'

'No, but I'd like to. He's always come to us, you see. He and Father are such old friends—they talk and talk ...' She broke off as there was a sudden commotion in front of them; a squealing of brakes, shouting and a dog's yelp. The car in front of them turned off the road, giving them a view of a group of people standing to stare at a little dog lying in the road. It tried to crawl away, yelped again, and lay still.

'Stop!' commanded Laura, and without waiting to see if her companion would do so, undid her seat belt and put an urgent hand on the door. Doctor van Meerum drew up smoothly, put out a restraining hand to stop her and said calmly, 'Stay where you are—I'll go and look.'

'Don't you dare leave him there!' she urged him fiercely. 'They drove on, the brutes—and look at all those miserable people, staring ...'

He didn't answer her, but got out of the car and crossed the street to where the dog lay, squatting on his heels to examine it and then picking it up carefully and carrying it back to the car, quite unheeding of the warning voices telling him that he would get bitten for his pains. The unhappy creature he held didn't look capable of biting anything or any-

16

one; Laura whisked the scarf from her neck and spread it on her knees, and opened the door to receive the stricken creature on to her lap.

'Hind legs broken,' said the doctor. 'Do you suppose there's a chance of patching him up in Casualty?'

Laura gave him a grateful look. 'Yes—the Sister in charge is a great friend of mine, she could hide us away somewhere ... could we hurry?' She put a gentle hand on the whimpering little creature. 'He must be in frightful pain. If only I'd seen who ran him down.' Her voice was wobbly with her rage and the doctor gave her a long look, although he said nothing as he got back into the car and drove with what speed he could to the hospital, where he drove round to Casualty entrance, told Laura to sit still and went inside, to return almost immediately with Sylvia Matthews. She greeted Laura with a cheerful: 'Hi there, ducky, what's all this about a casualty?' She cast an eye over the bedraggled little beast and grinned at the doctor beside her. 'A hushed-up job, I gather? Do you want to do it, sir, or shall I get the C.O.?'

'Oh, I'll do it, I think, Sister, then if there's any trouble I can deal with it. But we shall need someone to give the dope. Are you busy?'

'Not at the moment. There's an end cubicle you can have; whoever does the round hardly ever goes there, and if they do ...'

'I'll take the blame,' said the doctor easily, and opened the car door. 'Laura, it would be less painful for that little beast if you could manage to get out and hold him at the same time.'

She nodded and slid carefully out of the car and into Casualty, where, obedient to the doctor's advice, she sat down carefully again in the poky little cubicle at the end of the passage while one of the anaesthetists was fetched. He stared rather when he saw the patient and began an indignant: 'I say, Laura old girl, I can't ...' before he caught sight of Doctor van Meerum and stopped. 'Sorry, sir—you're the old man's—I should say, Mr Burnett's Dutch colleague, aren't you? We were told that you would be here.'

'Splendid,' murmured the doctor, and stripped off his jacket. 'If I could have an apron, and if you could knock this little chap out for long enough for us to set him to rights, I should be greatly obliged.' He smiled with great charm. 'I don't know your name ...'

'Clark, sir, Jeremy Clark. I'm with Mr Burnett for six months. I'll get the dope.'

To save the dog more pain, he rather gingerly put him under with Laura still holding him on her lap, but the moment the small creature had been transferred to the table she stood up, rolled up her sleeves and professed herself ready to help. 'I'm not on duty until eleven o'clock,' she explained, 'and if anyone comes, you can head them off, Sylvia.'

Her friend nodded. 'And there'll be coffee when you're through—in my office.' She whisked away with a wave of the hand and a conspirator's wink.

The dog's legs were miraculously clean breaks. Doctor van Meerum set them, put them into plaster and set about checking for other injuries. When finally he straightened his massive frame, he remarked: 'Nothing else, bar some bad bruising. What are we going to do with him?'

Jeremy spoke first. 'What about a dogs' home?'

'Certainly not!' exploded Laura. 'And he must surely belong to someone—ought we to advertise or tell the police, and I'll keep him in my room until ...'

The doctor interrupted her. 'I doubt if he belongs to anyone,' he observed, 'he's half starved and he hasn't a collar. I think, if you would agree, Laura, that he should come with me.'

The relief flooded over her face like a burst of sunshine. 'Oh, could he? But where will you keep him?' She frowned uncertainly. 'You can't have him with you, he'd be dreadfully in the way.'

'I'm staying with someone who I have no doubt will be glad to keep an eye on him if I have to leave him, and he should be well enough to travel to Birmingham with me.'

'Yes, but what will happen to him when you return to Holland?'

The doctor was washing his hands at the sink. 'I'll take him with me. I have an elderly sheepdog who will be delighted to have company.'

Laura heaved a sigh. 'Oh, won't that be nice for him,' she declared. 'But would you like me to have him now? He won't come round for a little while, will he?'.

'Quite soon, I should think. Would it not be better if someone were to find me a box or basket, and I'll keep him with me.'

'Aren't you addressing a post-graduate class, sir?' asked Jeremy doubtfully.

'Certainly I am, but I hardly think that this animal will disturb us.' He had put on his jacket and was standing placidly, waiting for someone to do as he had suggested. It was Laura who found a suitable box, lined it with old papers and a layer of tow and watched while the dog was laid gently into it. They had coffee then, although she didn't stay more than a few minutes, excusing herself on the grounds of getting into uniform after thanking the doctor for her lift and Sylvia for the coffee. She made no mention of seeing him again as she wished him goodbye and nor did he suggest it, but as she stooped to stroke the animal's matted head she said earnestly, 'Thank you for stopping and making him well again.'

He eyed her gravely. 'If I remember rightly, you ordered me to stop in no uncertain terms, although I can promise you that I would have done so even if you hadn't said a word.'

She smiled at him; she had a sweet smile, which just for a moment made her fleetingly pretty, although she was unaware of that. 'I shall hear how he goes on from Joyce,' she told him guilelessly.

Someone had brought her case in from the car and she picked it up as she went through Casualty, already filling up with minor cuts and burns, occasional fractures and dislocations; all the day-to-day cases. She glanced round her as she went; she wasn't likely to get anything sent up to the ward as far as she could see, although probably the Accident Room would keep her busy. She hoped so, for there was nothing like work for blotting out one's own thoughts and worries, and her head was full of both.

She climbed the stairs to her room in the Nurses' Home feeling alone and sad and sorry for herself, and cross too that she had allowed herself to give way to self-pity. As she unlocked the door and went into the pleasant little room she had made home for some years now, she bade herself stop behaving like a fool; she wasn't likely to see the doctor again and she would start, as from that very moment, to forget him.

CHAPTER TWO

SHE saw him exactly two hours later, for he accompanied Mr Burnett on his bi-weekly round, towering head and shoulders over everyone else. He wished her good morning with cool affability, remarked that they seemed to be seeing a good deal of each other that morning and added, 'The little dog is doing very nicely.'

'Oh, good.' Laura spoke warmly and then became a well-trained Sister again, leading the way to the first bed, very neat in her blue uniform with the quaint muslin cap perched on top of her neat head.

She handed Mr Burnett the first set of notes and advised him in her clear, pleasant voice: 'Mr Arthur True, facial injuries, concussion and severe lacerations of the upper right arm—admitted at eleven o'clock last night.'

Mr Burnett rumbled and mumbled to himself as he always did, cleared his throat and said, 'Ah, yes,' and turned to his registrar. 'You saw him, George? Anything out of the way?'

George White was earnest, painstaking and thoroughly reliable, both as a person and as a surgeon, and he was quite unexciting too. He gave his report with maddening slowness despite Mr Burnett's obvious desire for him to get on with it, so that Laura, aware of her chief's irritation, wasted no time in getting the patient ready for examination; no easy matter, for he was still semi-conscious and belligerent with it. But she coped with him quietly with a student nurse to help, and presently, when Mr Burnett had had a good look and muttered to Doctor van Meerum, his registrar and Laura, they moved on.

'Mr Alfred Trim,' Laura enlightened her audience, 'double inguinal hernia, stitches out yesterday.' She lifted the bedclothes and Mr Burnett stood studying his handiwork, apparently lost in admiration of it until he said finally: 'Well, we'll think about getting him home, Sister, shall we?' and swept on his way.

The next bed's occupant looked ill. 'Penetrating wound of chest,' stated Laura. 'I took the drain out an hour ago...' she added a few concise and rather bloodthirsty details and Mr Burnett frowned and said, 'Is that so?—we'll have a look.' He invited Doctor van Meerum to have a look too and they poked and prodded gently and murmured together with George agreeing earnestly with everything they said until Mr Burnett announced, 'We'll have him in theatre, Sister—five o'clock this afternoon.'

His gaze swept those around him, gathering agreement.

Five o'clock was a wretched time to send a case to theatre; Laura exchanged a speaking glance with her right hand. She was due off duty at that hour herself, and now it would be a good deal later than that, for Pat wouldn't be back from her afternoon until then and there would be a lengthy report to give. She checked a sigh and looking up, found Doctor van Meerum's dark eyes on her. He looked so severe that she felt guilty although she had no reason to be, and this made her frown quite fiercely, and when he smiled faintly, just as though he had know exactly what she had been thinking, she frowned even harder.

A tiresome man, she told herself strongly, walking into her life and turning it topsy-turvy, and whoever had made that silly remark about it being better to have loved and lost than never to have loved at all needed his head examined. She had been jogging along, not quite content, it was true, but at least resigned, and now she felt as though she had been hit by a hurricane which was blowing her somewhere she didn't want to go ...

She swept past the next bed, empty for the moment, and raised an eyebrow at the hovering nurse to draw the curtains around the next one in line. Old Mr Tyler, who had had a laparotomy two days previously—Mr Burnett had found what he had expected and worse besides, and Mr Tyler wasn't going to do. Laura looked at the tired old face with compassion and hoped, as she always did in like cases, that he would die in his sleep, and waited quietly while the surgeon chatted quietly with a convincing but quite false optimism. He drew Doctor van Meerum into the conversation too, and she listened to the big man saying just the right thing in his faultless English and liked him for it. She supposed she would have loved him whatever he was or did, but liking him was an extra bonus.

The next three patients were quickly dealt with; young men with appendices which had needed prompt removal and who, the moment they were fully conscious, set up a game of poker. Laura had obliged them with playing cards, extracted a promise from them not to gamble with anything more valuable than matches and propped them up in their chairs the moment they were pronounced fit to leave their beds. And here they sat for the greater part of their day, a little wan, but nicely diverted from worrying about their insides.

They greeted Mr Burnett in a cheerful chorus, assured him that they had never felt better, that Sister was an angel, and that they couldn't wait for the pleasure of having her remove their stitches. All of which remarks Laura took with motherly good nature, merely begging them to refrain from tiring themselves out before steering her party forward to the neighbouring bed. Its occupant, Mr Blake, was thin and middle-aged, and although his operation had been a minor one, a continuous string of complaints passed his lips all day and far into the night.

Mr Burnett, his entourage ranged behind him, stood by the bed and listened with an impassive face to details of uneatable porridge for breakfast, the callous behaviour of the house doctors and nurses, and Sister's cruelty in insisting that he should actually get up and walk to the bathroom. He shot her a look of great dislike as he spoke and Mr Burnett said quite sharply that since he was making such excellent progress he would do better to convalesce at home, where he would doubtless find nothing to grumble about. 'Though I doubt if you will find a better nurse or kinder person than Sister Standish,' he concluded severely.

He stalked away, muttering to himself, and Laura hastened to soothe him by pointing out the excellent progress the next patient was making.

'I don't know how you put up with it, Laura,' said Mr Burnett, half an hour later, when they were all squashed into her office drinking their coffee. 'For heaven's sake get married, girl, before you lose your wits. That Blake—I'll have him home tomorrow; he's fit enough, and besides taking up a bed he must be driving you all mad.'

'Well, that would be nice,' conceded Laura mildly, 'for he does wear one down, you know. But they're not all like that, you know, sir.'

He passed his cup for more coffee and snorted: 'If I wasn't a married man and old enough to be your father, I'd marry you myself just to get you out of this ward,' he assured her, and they all laughed, because Laura was considered to be one of the Sisters in the hospital whom no one could ever imagine leaving. Young but settled, the principal nursing officer had once described her, and Laura, who had heard of it through the hospital grapevine, had considered that it amounted to an insult.

They all got up to go presently, and Doctor van

Meerum, who had said very little anyway, merely murmured vague thanks in her general direction as he went through the door. She went and sat at her desk again when they had gone, doing absolutely nothing until Pat came to remind her that she had expressed a wish to inspect the previous day's operation cases.

She managed to forget the Dutch doctor more or less during the next few days; she had plenty of friends, she was popular in a quiet way and there was no reason for her to be lonely. And yet she was, and the loneliness was made worse when Joyce telephoned at the weekend and told her gleefully that Reilof van Meerum was spending it with them. 'We're going out to dinner,' she bubbled over the wire. 'I shall wear that blue dress—and on Sunday we're going out for the day in that super car of his. Laura, do you think he's rich?'

'I really don't know. Did he say anything about a dog?'

'Yes—rather a bind, really; he has to bring the creature with him, he says, because it's broken its legs. Still, I daresay we can dump it on someone.'

Laura didn't answer. Somehow the doctor hadn't struck her as being a man to opt out of something he had undertaken to do, and he had promised her ... She said mistakenly, 'It's only a very little dog.'

'How do you know?' asked Joyce after a tiny pause, and Laura, sighing for her unguarded tongue, told her, 'It was knocked down by a car just as we reached the hospital—we took it into Cas ...'

'Have you seen Reilof?'

'He did a round earlier in the week with Mr Burnett. I didn't talk to him at all—or rather, he didn't talk to me.'

She knew exactly what her young sister was thinking; that no man, no young, attractive man at any rate, would bother very much about a young woman who was looking thirty in the face. Thirty, to Joyce, was the absolute end.

Laura went home again at the end of the following week without having seen the doctor again, although she had found a note on her desk one morning to tell her that he had gone back to Holland, and that he had the little dog, now in excellent health albeit hating his plasters, with him. He was hers, RvM. She put the note away carefully and told herself once again to forget him.

Easier said than done, as it turned out, for when she did get home he was Joyce's main topic of conversation; they had had a super weekend and he was coming again just as soon as he could manage it. 'I've got him hooked,' declared Joyce happily. 'He's a bit old, but he's very distinguished, isn't he? and Uncle Wim says he's carved himself an excellent career—he's got a big practice somewhere near Hilversum. I imagine that the people who live round there are mostly well-off.' She added dreamily, 'I expect he's rich.' She smiled beguilingly at Laura. 'Look, be a darling—I don't dare to ask Uncle Wim any more questions, but you could, he dotes on you, and I do want to know.'

Laura shook her head; her godfather might dote on her, but he was the last person in the world to gossip about anyone. 'Why do you want to know so badly?' she asked.

Joyce grinned wickedly. 'I wouldn't mind being a doctor's wife, as long as he was very successful and had masses of money and I wouldn't have to do the housework or answer the door, like Doctor Wall's wife does in the village.'

Laura kept her voice matter-of-fact; Joyce fell in and out of love every few weeks, maybe her feeling for Doctor van Meerum was genuine, but on the other hand someone else might come along. 'Chance is a fine thing,' she remarked lightly, and wished with all her heart that she might have that chance.

'Like to bet on it?' Joyce looked like a charming kitten who'd got at the cream. 'I've bowled him over, you know; he's thirty-eight and he had a wife years ago, only she died, and now he's met me and discovered what he's been missing.'

Laura had been sitting in the window, perched on the open window sill, but she got up now, shivering a little; it was still a little chilly in the April sun, but that wasn't why she shivered. 'I must go and get tea,' she said. 'Are Father and Uncle Wim still playing chess?'

Joyce shrugged and yawned. 'How should I know? Why don't you go and see for yourself?'

In a way it was a relief to be back at work again,

although Laura loved being at home, but on the ward there was little time to bother with her own affairs. It was take-in week and the empty beds were filling fast, so that there was more than enough to do. She went her calm, sensible way, checking drips, seeing that the cases went on time to theatre and when they returned, were dealt with with all the skill available; and all the while being disturbed times out of number by housemen, George at his slowest, the Path Lab people, the lady social worker, and Mr Burnett, never at his sunniest during take-in week.

Moreover when she did escape to her office to catch up on her paper work, it was to be interrupted again by nurses wanting their days off changed, evenings when they had mornings, mornings when they had afternoons free ... she did her best to accommodate them, for she could remember her own student days and the agonising uncertainty of days off not fitting in with one's own private life. Staff was going to have a long weekend, which meant that Laura would be on call for a good deal of that period, something which she didn't mind about, for to go home and listen to Joyce eulogising about Reilof van Meerum was more than she could bear. It would be better, she reflected, when he had either gone for good or he and Joyce ... she tried not to think any more about that, but Joyce could be ruthless when she wanted something or someone.

It was a pity that her father had told her that she need not look for another job, she could stay home and do the housekeeping; he engaged a daily house-keeper at the same time, for as he was at pains to tell Laura, Joyce wouldn't be strong enough to cope with running the house on her own. And that meant that she would idle away her days, cooking up schemes with which to ensnare the doctor yet more deeply.

Laura went home the following weekend, and although her father had told her on the telephone that either he or Joyce would bring the car in to Chelmsford to meet her train, there was no one wait-ing, for her when she arrived. She waited for a little while and then telephoned home. Mrs Whittaker, the new housekeeper, answered. She sounded a dear soul but a little deaf and not at her best with the instrument, for she wasted a good deal of time saying 'Hullo', until Laura, getting in a word edgeways at last, asked for her father or Joyce. She had to repeat her question and when Mrs Whittaker finally grasped what she was saying, it was disappointing to be told that there was no one home.

Well, it had happened before. Laura left a mes-sage to say that she would get old Mr Bates to fetch her in his taxi from the village, and rang off. It took her a little while to get hold of him, and then she had had to wait half an hour for him to reach her, and she was tired and peevish by the time she opened the house door and went inside.

The hall was cool and dim, but the sitting room had a great many windows, allowing the spring sun-shine to pour into the room. There was no one there, though; she went through the house then, and found the kitchen empty too, with a note on the table 'Soup in saucepan', presumably meant for her. She went upstairs to her room next, unpacked her overnight bag, got into a rather elderly tweed skirt and a thin sweater and went downstairs again.

It was almost one o'clock by now and there was no sign of lunch or anyone to eat it; possibly her father and godfather had gone off on some expedition of their own and forgotten all about her arrival, but Joyce knew that she was coming. Laura hunted round the sitting room once more, looking for a note, and found none. She wandered into the kitchen, served herself some of the soup and sat down on the kitchen table, supping it from a bowl while she decided what she should do with her afternoon, for it looked as though she would have nothing but her own company for the next few hours.

But in this she was wrong; she had finished her soup and was sitting doing absolutely nothing, her head full of Reilof van Meerum, when the front door opened and she heard Joyce's voice, high and gay. She heard her father's voice too and then his rumbling laugh, and a moment later the kitchen door opened and her sister and the Dutch doctor came in.

Laura didn't get up, indeed she was too surprised to do so—Joyce hadn't mentioned that he would be there and just for a moment she could think of nothing at all to say. It was Joyce who spoke.

'Laura—oh, darling, I quite forgot that you were coming home.' She bit her lip and went on quickly: 'Daddy and Uncle Wim wanted to go to some fusty old bookshop and Reilof turned up—wasn't it lucky?—and took them in the car, and then we went for a drive—we've just had lunch at the Wise Man...' Her eyes fell on the empty bowl and she gave a charming little laugh. 'Oh, poor you—I told Mrs Whittaker not to bother because you'd probably not come ...'

The man beside her gave her a thoughtful glance and Laura saw it and said at once: 'My fault, I usually telephone, don't I—I changed my mind at the last minute and got Bates to fetch me from the station.' She smiled at her sister. 'I wasn't hungry, anyway.' She turned the smile on the doctor. 'Hullo —how's the little dog?'

He answered her gravely: 'He's fine. I had to leave him at home, of course, but my housekeeper is his slave and will take good care of him.' He paused for a moment. 'If I had known that you were coming home this weekend I would have given you a lift.'

Very civil, thought Laura, even though he was dying to get Joyce to himself; he could hardly keep his eyes off her, and indeed her sister looked delightful in a new suit and those frightfully expensive shoes she had wheedled out of her father. 'And my new Gucci scarf,' thought Laura indignantly, suddenly aware that her own clothes did nothing to enhance her appearance.

33

She got down from the table then, saying in a bright voice: 'I'm going along to see Father and Uncle Wim—what happened to Mrs Whittaker?'

Joyce's blue eyes were like a child's, wide and innocent. 'I told her to take the rest of the day off. Laura darling, I do feel awful ...' and Laura thought without anger: 'If she weren't my sister, I would believe her, too.'

'You see,' Joyce went on, 'Daddy and Uncle Wim are going to Doctor Wall's for dinner—his wife will be at the W.I. meeting and Reilof is taking me to that gorgeous place at Great Waltham ...'

'And we shall be delighted if you would join us,' the doctor interrupted her gently.

He was kind, thought Laura; he might have dozens of faults, but lack of kindness wasn't one of them. 'That's sweet of you,' she replied hastily, allowing her voice to show just sufficient regret, 'but actually I've reams of things to do and I was looking forward to an evening on my own.' For good measure she added, 'We've had a pretty hectic time on the ward.'

'Poor old Laura,' Joyce spoke with facile sympathy, 'but if that's what you want to do ...'

Laura considered for one wild moment telling Joyce what she really wanted to do, and then looking up she found the doctor's dark, questioning gaze upon her, so that she hastily rearranged her features into a vague smile and said enthusiastically, 'Oh, rather. There's nothing like a quiet evening, you know.' She prolonged the smile until she reached the door, said ' 'bye' to no one in particular and left them together.

The house was very quiet when everyone had gone out that evening; her father had pressed her to go with them to the doctor's, but if she had done so the three old friends would have felt bound to exert themselves to entertain her, whereas she knew well enough that they wanted nothing better than to mull over the latest medical matters. So she repeated her intention of staying at home, saw the two elder gentlemen out of the front door and a few minutes later did the same for her sister and Doctor van Meerum. Joyce looked radiant and the doctor looked like a man who had just won the pools. She went back indoors, shutting the door firmly behind her, and wandered into the kitchen to get herself some supper. Scrambled eggs, rather watery because she cried all over them.

But no one would have known that a few hours later; she sat, composed and restful, in the sitting room, her newly washed hair hanging in a shining mousy cloud down her back, the coffee tray and sandwiches set ready, the local paper on her lap. The older gentlemen got back first, as was to be expected; they had drunk most of the coffee and made great inroads upon the sandwiches before they were joined by Joyce and Reilof van Meerum. Joyce glowed, looking quite breathtakingly lovely— enough to turn any man's head, and it was obvious that that was what had happened to the doctor—he wasn't a man to show his feelings, but some feelings couldn't be concealed. Laura went away to get more coffee and when she returned he took the tray from her, asked her kindly if she had enjoyed her evening, and expressed the hope that she would be free to join them on the following day.

Laura, aware of Joyce's anxious wordless appeal to say no, said with genuine regret and a complete absence of truth that she had promised to go back early as she was spending the afternoon with friends. The doctor's polite regret sounded genuine enough but hardly heartfelt, and later, when they had parted for the night, she wasn't surprised when Joyce came to her room.

'Thank heaven I caught your eye,' she observed. 'Heavens, suppose you'd said yes!' She smiled sunnily. 'He was only being polite, you know. We're going out for the day—to Cambridge—he was there, simply ages ago.' She settled herself on the end of the bed. 'Laura, isn't it super—I'm sure he's going to ask me to marry him.'

Laura was plaiting her hair at the dressing table and didn't turn round; although she had been expecting Joyce to tell her just that, now that she heard the actual words she didn't want to believe them. She finished the plait with fingers which trembled and said carefully: 'Is he? However do you know?'

Joyce laughed, 'Silly—of course I do,' and she added with unconscious cruelty: 'But you wouldn't know ...'

Laura smiled ruefully. 'No, I wouldn't. And are you going to say yes?'

'Of course—lord, Laura, I'd be a fool if I didn't—he's very good-looking and he adores me and I'm sure he's got plenty of money although he hasn't exactly said so—but he's got that marvellous car and his clothes are right.'

Laura stared unseeingly at her reflection in the looking-glass. Her face, she was thankful to see, looked just the same, although inside she was shaking with indignation and rage and a hopeless grief. 'Do you love him?' she asked.

Joyce got off the bed and strolled to the door. 'Darling, I'm prepared to love anyone who can give me all the pretty things I want.' She paused before she closed the door behind her. 'I suppose he turns me on, if that'll satisfy you.'

Laura got up early the next morning. She had slept badly and the urge to get out of the house before anyone else got downstairs was strong. She got into slacks and a blouse and went, quiet as a mouse, downstairs. Breakfast was already laid in the dining room, but she went straight to the kitchen, made tea, cut a slice of bread and butter to go with it and fetched a jacket from behind the kitchen door. It was a splendid morning as only an early May morning can be and she went through the village and then turned off down the narrow lane which was the back way to the neighbouring village. It had high banks on either side of it and the birds were already there, singing. There were catkins and lambs-tails too, and the hedges were thick with bread and cheese, green and fresh, and tucked away here and there were clumps of primroses and patches of violets.

The lane wound a good deal, so that it took twice as long as it needed to to reach Masham, but she had time and to spare; Joyce and Reilof van Meerum weren't likely to leave the house much before ten o'clock, and Laura had just heard the church bells, still quite a way away, ringing for eight o'clock service. She reached the first few cottages as a handful of people came out of the church with the rector on their heels. He saw her at once and greeted her with pleasure, for they had known each other all her life.

'Laura—you've strayed into the wrong parish, but how nice. It's early, though.' He gave her a questioning look.

'I've got a weekend,' she told him, 'and it's such a lovely morning, I simply couldn't waste it in bed. I love the walk through the lane.'

He nodded. 'Peaceful and quiet, designed for thinking one's own thoughts.' He gave her a quick glance, taking in the pallor of a sleepless night and her unhappy eyes. 'Come and have breakfast with Martha and me,' he begged her, 'the house is so quiet now that Guy's up at Cambridge.'

He led the way down the village street and across to the white house at the end of it. A charming house, built in the days when the village parson had half a dozen children and needed the rooms. Now, as Laura knew, it was almost empty and a well-loved millstone round the rector's neck. They went in through the kitchen door and found Mrs Lamb frying bacon at the old-fashioned stove, and presently they all sat down to a leisurely meal before Mr Lamb got on to his bicycle and went off to a hamlet nearby to take morning service, leaving Laura to help with the washing up, peel the potatoes for lunch and set the table.

It was almost eleven o'clock by the time she got home, and time to get a meal for her father and godfather. She found them walking in the garden, deep in some conversation or other. They greeted her absentmindedly, asked vaguely if she was going to make them some coffee, and resumed their perambulations, leaving her to go to her room, change into a suit, do her hair and return to the kitchen. She gave them their coffee presently and then set about getting lunch, and it was over this meal that her father mentioned that Joyce and the doctor had left directly after breakfast and didn't expect to get back until after tea. 'They seem to be greatly interested in each other,' he observed, 'although I think myself that Reilof is too old for my little Joyce —still, if the child wants him, I'll not say no—he's obviously greatly taken with her.' He glanced at Laura across the table. 'I daresay you've noticed, my dear?'

She said yes, she had, her voice placid, and went on to remind him that she would be going back on the three o'clock train, whereupon he offered to drive her to the station. 'It will be a nice little run for your godfather, too,' he said with satisfaction, and added a little anxiously: 'How about our tea, my dear—and supper?'

'Tea's all ready on a tray on the kitchen table, Father, you·only have to boil a kettle. It's cold supper, on the top shelf of the fridge, but I should think Joyce would be back by then. I'll lay up another tray after I've washed up, though, just in case she isn't.'

The matter being settled, she got on with the chores, repacking her bag once more before going in search of her father to remind him that he was taking her into Chelmsford. She sat with her godfather on the back seat because he complained mildly that he had seen almost nothing of her, and presently she wished she had insisted on him sitting with her father, because the questions he put to her were a little disconcerting and far too searching. Was she happy at the hospital? Had she any plans for the future, had she a young man?—an old-fashioned term which hardly fitted the circumstances, she considered, half amused. And what did she think of Reilof van Meerum?

She hedged round the last question. She didn't know him well—he seemed very nice, but how could she know ...?

'You don't need to know anything about anybody,' stated her godfather, 'either you like them or you don't.' He gave her a sidelong glance. 'You do, Laura?'

'Well, yes, Uncle Wim.' She hastened to give the conversation another turn. 'You'll be here when I come home again—I'm not sure when . . .?'

'I'll be here—I shall go back with Reilof, but he comes so frequently I have no plans at present but shall fit in with him.'

'Then I shall see you again.' She checked, just in time, a sigh of relief as her father came to a halt before the station entrance, then she bent to kiss her companion and bade him stay where he was as she got out. She retrieved her bag, kissed her father too, and hurried away to catch her train. She spent the journey wondering what Joyce and Reilof were doing; Joyce had been very sure of him—any time now, thought Laura unhappily, I shall get a message to say that they're going to get married. She gazed out of the window, seeing nothing of the rather dreary fringe of London and wishing she could be miles away, so that she couldn't be telephoned, then she would never know—no, that would be far worse. The sooner she knew the better. Then she could start to forget Reilof as the man she had fallen in love with, and think of him as a future brother-in-law. The idea appalled her.

CHAPTER THREE

LAURA was sitting in Ann Matthew's room, drinking tea and joining in, in an absent manner, the end-of-day talk. Ann had Women's Surgical and had been on duty for the weekend, as had several other of Laura's friends, and she had been greeted with the news that there had been a minor train accident that morning with a large number of light injuries to be dealt with as well as several cases to be warded.

'Sunday morning,' protested Audrey Crewe, who ran the Accident Room with the efficient nonchalance of an expert and was the envy of every student nurse who worked for her. 'The one time in the week when I can really get down to the wretched off-duty and have two cups of coffee in a row—they poured in, ducky, and so dirty, poor souls—though most of them only had cuts and bruises and shock. I had to send four up to you, though, Laura—they'll keep you busy for a day or two; two have had surgery, the others won't be done until tomorrow, they're not fit enough.'

'It's news like that that brings me rushing back,' remarked Laura tartly, and was instantly sorry she had said it, because someone asked, 'Why did you come back this afternoon, Laura? You usually sneak in at the last possible moment.'

42

'Well, Joyce was out for the day, and the earlier train fitted in with Father's plans ...'

'Go on with you,' said a voice from the door. 'You've quarrelled with the boy-friend. You're wanted on the telephone, love—I expect he wants to make it up.'

There was a little outburst of laughter as Laura went out of the door, and she laughed with them while her insides went cold. It would be Joyce, to tell her that she was going to marry Reilof van Meerum, and she was so certain of it that when she heard her sister's excited voice telling her just that, it wasn't a shock at all, just a numbness which gripped her brain and her tongue so that Joyce asked sharply:

'Laura? Are you still there? Why don't you say something?'

'It's marvellous news,' she managed then, her voice calm and pleasantly surprised, 'and I hope you'll both be very happy. Does Father know?'

'Yes,' bubbled Joyce, 'and so does Uncle Wim, but you know what old people are, they hum and ha and sound so doubtful ...'

'Well, as long as neither of you is doubtful, I shouldn't think there was anything to worry about, darling.'

'We've opened a bottle of champagne—isn't it all wildly exciting? Reilof's here—he wants to speak to you.'

Laura drew a long breath and thanked heaven silently that she didn't have to meet him face to face.

At least by the time they did meet again she would have her feelings well in hand. All the same, when she heard his quiet 'Laura?' in her ear, she had to wait a second before she could get out a matter-of-fact 'hullo'.

'Aren't you going to congratulate me?' he asked.

'Of course, with all my heart.'

'That's nice to hear. I'm sure you're going to be a delightful sister-in-law. A pity that you aren't here to celebrate with us. You must be sure and have a free weekend next time I come over.'

'Oh, rather.' Laura was aware that she sounded far too hearty, she would be babbling if she wasn't careful, any minute now her tongue would run away with her. 'Such a pity I had to come back early,' she chattered brightly, 'but I'd promised ages ago . . .'

His 'Oh, yes?' sounded faintly amused and a little bored; she was wasting his time, time he could be spending with Joyce. She held the mouthpiece a little way from her and called: 'Okay, I'm coming now,' and then spoke into it again. 'So sorry, someone's waiting for me—have a glass of champagne for me, won't you? See you soon. 'Bye!'

She hung up and went slowly back up the stone staircase, not going back to Ann's room but into her own. But that wouldn't do, sooner or later someone would come looking for her. She snatched up a towel and sponge and went into one of the bathrooms and turned on the taps, and presently when a voice asked her if she was in there, she was able to answer quite cheerfully that the telephone call had taken so long that it hadn't seemed worthwhile going back to them all.

'Not bad news, I hope?' asked the voice anxiously.

She forced her voice into just the right tones of pleased excitement: 'Lord, no. Marvellous, actually —Joyce has got engaged. I'll tell you all about it later.'

Later was breakfast, a blessedly hurried meal, so that she barely had the time to repeat the news baldly, listen to the excited babble of talk when someone realised that Reilof was the dishy doctor who had been seen with Mr Burnett, admit that he had been visiting her home quite regularly for the past week or so, and gobble her toast before the hurried race to the wards.

The four new cases kept her busy all day; none of them was very well and the two who were to go to theatre had to be prepped and doped and reassured, and once they had been wheeled away on their trolleys, there was everything to set in readiness for their return to the ward. Their wives came too, hurrying in from their surburban homes, leaving heaven alone knew what chaos behind them, to be sat in Laura's office, given tea and sympathy and reassured in their turn. Presently, when they had calmed down, she took them along to the visitors' room where they could sit in some comfort, with magazines to read and coffee and sandwiches served from time to time, although in Laura's experience the magazines were rarely opened and the sand-

45

wiches and coffee were returned untouched.

And this time it was worse than usual, for one of the men died only a short time after he had been returned to the ward from the Recovery Room; a sudden collapse which all their skills couldn't cure. Laura, instead of going off duty, stayed with the bereaved wife until relations came to take her home, and then went over to the home, to her own room, so tired that she no longer had any very clear thoughts left in her head. Ann gave her a mug of tea after she had had her bath and she barely gave herself time to drink it before falling into bed and sleeping at once.

But the rest of the week was better than that. The other three men improved rapidly, the poker players, their stitches out, went home, sheepishly offering her a large bunch of flowers as they went, and Mr Bates, to her great astonishment, gone home a week or more, returned one morning to offer his grudging thanks for the care he had received while he had been in the ward. Laura was so surprised that she could only stare at him and then, realising what an effort it must have been for him to have made such a gesture, she took him into the ward to see one or two of the patients he had known. They weren't all that pleased to see him, for he had been unpopular with his fellow sufferers, but as one of them pointed out to Laura afterwards, his visit relieved the tedium of the long hospital morning.

She was on duty that weekend, and towards the end of the week following it she telephoned Joyce and invented a mythical friend who had invited her out, for her sister had telephoned her earlier in the week to tell her that Reilof van Meerum would be coming once more, and made it clear that if Laura were to go home it would spoil their outings together, for he would be sure to invite her along too, out of politeness.

'And I don't see much of him, darling, do I?' Joyce's voice sounded vaguely discontented, and it was then that Laura had determined to make some excuse to stay in London, and on the Friday she telephoned to say that the girl from Physiotherapy who had got married a few months previously had asked her to spend the weekend ...

Joyce wasn't really interested. 'Oh, lovely for you,' she observed carelessly. 'Reilof's coming next weekend too—flying over—but of course you won't be free, will you?'

Laura said no and what a pity, knowing that Joyce would have been furious if it had been otherwise. 'But I'm coming home the weekend after that,' she warned, 'because I want some summer clothes from my room.'

It was after she had rung off that she decided to see what could be done about changing her days for that particular weekend—she could have Friday instead of Saturday; Reilof usually arrived on a Friday evening, but she could be gone by then. Really it would be a relief when they were married and living in Holland and she could settle down to her usual home visits.

She sighed. They wouldn't be the same any more,

a reflection which did nothing to lighten her heavy heart. She turned her attention to the papers on her desk and resolutely closed her mind to her own affairs.

She hated staying in London over the weekend, it seemed such a dreadful waste of her free days, for of course the girl from Physiotherapy had been nothing but an invention ... still, she made the best of it by going to see a collection of pictures she had been told were well worth a visit, doing a little shopping and going in the evening to the cinema with George, who, although dull and a thought pompous, was at least company. He took her to an intense film she couldn't understand because it was Italian and she suspected that the dubbing wasn't anything like the original script. Besides, he kept up a low-voiced monologue in her ear, describing just how he had removed a very nasty cyst from a man's shoulder—it was more of a mutter, actually, and too soft for anyone else to hear, but all the same she felt acutely uncomfortable about it. He took her to supper afterwards, too, and over their sausages and chips gave her a lecture on antibiotics.

She considered that, on the whole, she had earned both film and supper; probably George would make some girl a kind husband one day, but it was such a pity that he had no sense of humour. Probably Reilof van Meerum had none, either; she didn't know him well enough to discover that, but she was quite certain that George wouldn't have stopped in the middle of a busy street to pick up a little mongrel dog which had been run over, and certainly he would never have dreamed of taking it to Cas. To a vet, yes, where he would, give him his due, have paid any fees necessary and then, his duty done, washed his hands off it.

The week went slowly and when she telephoned home it was her godfather who answered, assuring her that he intended to stay another week or so and asking if she would be home for the weekend. 'For we see little enough of you,' he reminded her gently.

Laura told him that yes, she would be coming, but forbore from saying that her visit would be for a few hours only on Friday. She would be able to think of some excuse when the time came, she decided hopefully, as she made some vague reply to his invitation to visit him later on in the year. She would have to wait and see about that; Uncle Wim lived close to Reilof van Meerum, although she wasn't sure just how often they saw each other, but there was the ever-present risk of meeting Joyce and Reilof and she didn't think she would be able to bear that. Later on perhaps, when she had learned to school her feelings.

She caught an early morning train on Friday without telling anyone she was coming and she didn't phone Bates till she got to Chelmsford, because he was quite capable of telling her father, who would probably tell Joyce to upset all her plans and make her furious. But Bates, when he arrived, showed no curiosity as to her movements; he had a wedding on his hands that afternoon, and his talk was all of that.

It was beginning to rain as she went up the garden path, and the house, with its door closed, looked forlorn. It was barely eleven o'clock; she had plenty of time to get her things, but she would first find her father. His study was empty, so was the sitting room, and there was no Mrs Whittaker in the kitchen. Rather puzzled, Laura went upstairs and was relieved to hear the radio playing in Joyce's room. She hurried her steps a little and opened the door and stopped short.

Joyce was standing in the middle of the room, the contents of her wardrobe spread out around her on the bed, the chairs and open drawers. Her case, the expensive one her father had given her for her last birthday, was open on the bed, half packed.

She looked up quickly as Laura opened the door, her pretty mouth open in surprise, her eyes wide. She said: 'It's only Friday—you never come home on Friday.'

'No,' said Laura, 'I don't—but now I'm here, although no one else is. Where is everyone, Joyce?'

'Father and Uncle Wim have gone to those gardens—you know, they're open now—I suggested it,' Joyce spoke defiantly, 'and Mrs Whittaker wanted to go to a wedding.'

'You're going away?' Laura made her voice casual, feeling her way cautiously—perhaps Joyce had quarrelled with Reilof. It struck her suddenly that it wasn't that at all, she was going to him ...

Her sister folded a skirt, her pretty mouth sulky. 'Yes, I am, and since you're here, poking your nose into my affairs, you can jolly well help.'

Laura pushed some clothes on one side and sat down on the bed. 'Look, love, what's the matter? Don't you want a village wedding? I know Father is keen on you having one, but you only have to say so—— Are you going off with Reilof somewhere quiet to get married? You only had to say so, you know.' She shook out a crumpled blouse and folded it carefully. 'If you'd explained what you wanted...'

Joyce laughed. 'You're so silly, Laura, I suppose that's because you're getting on a bit. I'm going away all right, but not with Reilof. Oh, he's all right, I suppose, he would have given me everything I asked for, and I would have turned into a good little housewife with a string of noisy kids.' She gave a little laugh. 'He likes children, did you know?' She flung a dressing gown on top of everything else and closed the case. 'I'm going to America with someone I met a couple of weeks ago—he's got a special licence and we're getting married at the Registrar's Office in Bishop's Stortford.' She glanced at her watch. 'In about an hour's time. He's fabulously rich and he likes a good time and he loves me madly.'

Laura had listened to this astonishing speech with a sense of unreality so strong that she pinched her arm to make sure that she wasn't dreaming. 'Reilof...' she managed. 'But you said you loved him—he thinks you're going to marry him—he's coming here this evening—you can't...'

'Who says I can't? I'm going to do what I like with

my life, Laura, and get the most out of it, too. Reilof's almost middle-aged, and I'd have settled for him because there wasn't any one else around with his kind of money, but now Larry has turned up, it's different.' Joyce was putting on her coat now. 'You can tell him, Laura—I've written him a letter, of course, and you can give it to him and explain it at the same time. You can tell Daddy too.'

'I won't.' Laura was surprised to find herself shaking with rage.

'All right, don't—I don't care; let them find out for themselves.'

'Joyce, you can't do it; Father will be so upset, and what about Reilof?'

'Father won't be upset for long, you know he always lets me do what I like, and Reilof...' She shrugged her shoulders. 'There are plenty more girls.' She picked up her case and crossed the room to give Laura a perfunctory kiss. 'There's the taxi. Wish me luck.'

Laura suppressed a wish to burst into tears. She said gently, 'I hope you'll be very happy, darling, even though you've made Reilof very unhappy. You'll write or telephone, won't you? Father won't be happy until he hears from you. And what about Reilof?'

'He can take care of himself—really, Laura, he's not a baby, you know. I daresay I'll telephone later. 'Bye for now.'

She had gone, leaving the room in complete disorder.

Laura started to tidy up, her movements automatic as she put discarded clothing neatly back into drawers and cupboards, trying to make her mind tackle the situation. Presently, with everything neat and tidy again, she sat down on the bed, the better to think.

It was no good giving way to concern for Reilof, it was important that she should tackle the deplorable affair as impersonally as possible. She remembered that Reilof never arrived before the evening and there was no reason to suppose that he would do anything different now; she would be able to tell her father and leave him to explain when the doctor got to the house. 'Man to man,' she told herself out loud, 'that should be much easier—I'll give Father the letter too, then if Reilof wants to he can go back home at once.' The home he had expected to share with Joyce, her heart reminded her; his plans shattered, heaven only knew what plans he had made. He had given Joyce a ring too—Laura hadn't seen it, but her sister had telephoned her in order to describe it at great length. A solitaire diamond in a modern setting; she had been jubilant about it, especially as Reilof had wanted her to wear what she described as some dreary old ruby thing which just everyone in his family had worn at some time or other. But she had twisted him round her thumb easily enough, she had added gleefully, and Laura would be able to see it next time she came home.

'Well, I am home,' said Laura worriedly, talking to herself again, 'and a pretty kettle of fish it is. I wish Father would come home.' She heaved a sigh as the front door opened and shut. She snatched up Joyce's letter and raced down the stairs, to stop two-thirds of the way down, because it wasn't her father but Reilof standing there, looking up at her.

He smiled, 'Hullo, I didn't expect to see you, Laura,' but when she just went on standing there, her earnest, ordinary face the picture of surprised woe, the smile disappeared and his dark brows drew together in a questioning frown. 'Something is the matter? Joyce?'

Laura nodded; it was a funny thing, she reflected; on the ward she was capable of dealing with any situation, however sticky, which might crop up, but now she hadn't a clue how to begin. She went on gaping at him, feeling a slow resentment that she should have been forced into such a wretched situation. If it had been anyone else—a man she didn't know well—but Reilof, whom she loved and was powerless to help—it was past bearing.

'Well, supposing you tell me?' Reilof had taken off his car coat and flung it into a chair, now he lounged against the door, his hands in his pockets, no expression at all upon his handsome face.

She swallowed. 'Joyce asked me to give you this.' She watched his face anxiously as he walked over to her and took the envelope from her hand. It hadn't changed at all, it looked calm, even placid, and remained so as he opened the envelope and took out the letter within. When he had finished reading it, he folded it neatly and put it back.

54

'Did you know about this?' he inquired, and his voice was very even.

'Not until I came home about an hour ago—less than that. Joyce was—was just leaving. You see, she didn't expect me.'

'And your father?' He sounded politely interested, no more.

'He and Uncle Wim—well, Joyce suggested that they went to those botanical gardens—she didn't want them to know . . . I hoped they would be back . . . I didn't expect you'd be here until this evening.'

His smile held a faint sneer. 'Poor big sister Laura, left with the task of breaking the news.' His voice held bitterness now. 'You didn't do it very well.'

This annoyed her, and she said with some spirit, 'Well, if you must know, I was going to explain to Father and he would have told you.' She added idiotically, 'Man to man.'

The smile became a short derisive laugh. 'Oh, but I much prefer woman to man—sympathy, the tender touch and all the rest of it.'

My goodness, thought Laura, he's in a rage for all that calm face. She asked doubtfully, 'Are you going to go after her? I don't expect they've . . .'

'Got married yet? You silly girl, of course I'm not going after Joyce.' He looked away for a minute. 'It's hardly my intention to drag her back by the hair of her lovely head—and she's quite right, of course, I am too old for her.'

Laura gasped. 'She didn't say that? But it isn't

true—you're thirty-eight, aren't you? That's not old.'

'Perhaps not to you, Laura, but Joyce is only twenty.'

She went a little pale at his unthinking unkindness, but she said steadily: 'Age doesn't have anything to do with it.'

He raised his eyebrows. 'Oh, how would you know about that?'

'That's twice you've been abominably rude,' she pointed out. 'It's all right, though—I know you're angry and shocked and unhappy. I—I think I understand a little of how you feel; you'd like to knock someone down, I expect, but there's no one here, only me, and I shouldn't let you.'

The sneer was there once more. 'Indeed? And how could you prevent me from doing so?'

'Never you mind.' She came down off the stairs at last and said carefully, 'Reilof, there are a great many other girls—pretty girls—in the world. I know that seems a dreadful thing to say, but it's true. Once you've got over this ...'

His dark eyes, so hard that she winced, swept over her. 'My dear good girl,' and his voice was almost a drawl, 'she wouldn't need to be pretty; anyone will do after Joyce, there couldn't be another girl like her.' He laughed without humour. 'Good God, girl, if it comes to that, I might just as well marry you.'

'Then why don't you?' asked Laura, very much to her own astonishment. She hadn't meant to say that at all, the words had popped out, and now there was no way of getting them back again. She lifted her firm little chin and met his dark look.

If he was astonished too, he didn't show it. 'Indeed, and why not?' he echoed smoothly, 'since I'm obviously too—er—mature for Joyce, then I must learn my lesson from her, mustn't I, and take someone nearer my own age.' His eyes narrowed. 'And you, Laura, are reaching thirty, are you not?'

He was being deliberately cruel now, but she could understand that; he wanted to hit back and she was the nearest thing to hit. She agreed in a quiet voice but made no other comment, and presently he went on:

'We're both old enough not to expect romance, I imagine. At least I am cured of that illusion, although I must admit that having made up my mind to marry again, the prospect of remaining single for the rest of my life doesn't appeal to me any more.' He took his hands from his pockets and came towards her, his voice quite kind now.

'A marriage of friends, Laura, nothing more—I want no more of romance; companionship, someone to run my home and entertain my guests and friends, that will suffice for me. And what about you? Is that enough for you too? Or do you want to go on waiting patiently for the man of your dreams to come along?'

She shook her head. 'I can promise you I shan't do that,' she assured him seriously. 'You only have to take a good look at me—nudging thirty and what my mother always described as homely. And even if my dream man came along, he would hardly take a second glance at me, would he?'

He nodded in agreement and she thought what a preposterous conversation they were having.

'Then you would marry me?'

'Yes,' said Laura baldly.

He studied her at length. 'You're very certain. Why?'

It would have been nice to have been able to answer him truthfully, instead she said soberly: 'Mr Burnett was quite right, you know; the prospect of being a Ward Sister for the rest of my working life quite appals me. I've been nursing for ten years now and I love it, make no mistake about that, but it's a narrow life and an exacting one, and there are so many things I want to do and so far I've never had enough time to do much of any of them.'

'For instance?'

She was aware that he was only giving her his polite attention while the rest of his mind was given over to the shattering news she had just given him, but she went on talking, knowing that the only way to treat an abnormal situation was to be as normal as possible. A pretended normality, but at least it kept one from an outburst of rage which one might regret later. Children were lucky, she thought inconsequently, they could express their feelings exactly as they wished, whereas here was Reilof, and for that matter, herself too, both shocked and unhappy though for different reasons, and all they could do was have this ridiculous conversation.

'Petit-point,' she murmured, and when he smiled faintly, 'reading all the books I've ever wanted to, having a garden and tending it and picking the flowers and arranging them—taking hours over it —and meeting people—oh, I meet people every day; doctors and nurses and patients, and we all talk about the same thing, each from our own point of view. I want to meet people who know things— like Uncle Wim ...'

She thought that he hadn't been listening, but now he gave her a considering look and she wondered if, just for a moment, he had forgotten Joyce. 'And if we were to marry you would be content with such simple pleasures as these? No holidays abroad, no theatres and dances and dinner parties—you wouldn't expect me to change my selfish bachelor ways to suit you?'

'Would you have changed them for Joyce?'

His face was bleak. 'Of course—it's different when one loves someone. One wants to please them, to make them happy.'

Rather a poor outlook for me, thought Laura, and said calmly, 'No, I'd not bother you—I'd be there if you wanted me, though.'

His mouth twisted and she went on quickly, 'It's not what you'd hoped for, but it might be better than being lonely for the rest of your life.' She went on in a matter-of-fact tone, 'But there, I daresay you don't mean a word of it—one says things when one is angry or upset.'

He interrupted her brusquely. 'I mean every

word, Laura. I'm not at all sure of my reasons, but I do mean what I've said. But you—you must have time to think it over; I stand to gain a hostess for my friends, someone to run my home, bear me company, but you gain very little—a disgruntled man, disappointed in love and used until recently to leading a solitary life. There may be days when you'll hate me and wish that you'd never married me.'

He paused to look at her and she said placidly, 'Very likely,' while her heart cried silently, 'Never that,' and presently he went on: 'Would you consider giving in your notice at St Anne's—that would give you a month or so to make up your mind.'

'Very well.' It was time this extraordinary conversation was brought to a close, and she asked politely: 'Would you like a cup of tea? You must be tired after your journey.'

He let out a bellow of laughter. 'Not tired, Laura, but I'll have your cup of tea. Is it not supposed to be the panacea of all ills?'

CHAPTER FOUR

BACK in St Anne's that Saturday night, Laura, so late in that all her friends were in bed and asleep, made no attempt to go to bed herself, but sat in the small easy chair provided for each Sister's comfort, by her window. There was nothing to see; it was pitch dark and even in daylight the view was nothing but chimneypots and rather shabby slate roofs, and anyway, she wasn't looking at anything. Her brain was busy going over the events of her stay at home. Because of course she had stayed—she hadn't intended to, but there was no point in rushing off again now that Joyce's departure was a known fact, and it might have looked as though she was chickening out of an unpleasant situation. So she stayed and cooked supper for them all while her father and Reilof had gone to the study and Uncle Wim had kept her company in the kitchen, getting dreadfully in the way and talking about everything under the sun except the one topic uppermost in her mind, until at length she had asked: 'Godfather, what do you think? I mean about Joyce and Reilof—he must be broken-hearted.'

Her elderly companion had settled himself more comfortably in the shabby old chair by the Aga, Mittens on his knee. 'For the moment, my dear—

only for the moment. You see, love and infatuation are rather alike to begin with.'

Laura stirred her soup. 'You mean he didn't—doesn't love her?'

'Shall we say that he thought he did, and still thinks so, and what man would not? Such a pretty girl with all that lovely golden hair and those eyes—but of course it isn't eyes and hair which count in the long run, Laura, and after a while a man comes to his senses and realizes that.'

'Oh, does he? And how does one tell the difference?'

'My dear child, you ask me that when you already know the answer.'

'Me?'

'Have you not known the difference between your love for Reilof and Joyce's infatuation for him, or rather for the things he could give her—striking good looks, the assurance of an older man, money—although she wasn't quite certain about that, was she?—and the satisfaction of being adored by a man of the world?'

Laura hardly heard the last bit of his remark. 'My love for Reilof,' she uttered. 'Godfather . . .'

'Oh, don't worry, Laura, no one else even guesses, and certainly not Reilof. You have no need to look so alarmed.'

She was at the table preparing bread for croutons, and paused, knife in hand, to ask, 'But you knew?'

'Well, yes, but then you and I have always been close, have we not? I think of you as my own daughter, and perhaps I know a good deal more about you than you do yourself.'

She popped her bread cubes into the pan and watched them crisp. 'Uncle Wim, this may sound crazy to you, but he's asked me to marry him. We were talking and he was so angry, although he didn't look angry, if you know what I mean, and he said he might as well marry anyone if he couldn't marry Joyce, so I said, well, why not me? And—and he agreed in a nasty smooth voice and we talked about that for a bit too, and then I said I supposed he'd been talking wildly, but he said no, he hadn't, and I might as well give a month's notice at St Anne's and think about it and let him know ... He only wants a companion and someone to run his home, he says he's done with romance.'

She had dished the croutons and lifted her saucepan lids and peered inside, prodding their contents with a fork.

'Of course he has, we all say that at such times, it's a very natural reaction,' her godparent had observed comfortably. 'It happens time and time again. You will of course accept.'

Laura remembered how quickly she had said yes, she would.

She undressed then and got into bed, her brain still busy. Joyce had telephoned late on Friday evening and had contrived, as only she could, to wring forgiveness out of her father, even a reluctant acceptance of her actions; she was deliriously happy, she had said. Larry was super and although they would be flying to America in a few days she would bring him home before they went, and anyway, he was so rich that she would be able to come home and see them all just whenever she wanted to.

She didn't mention Reilof at all, and Laura, who had whisked him off to the kitchen when the telephone rang, kept him at the sink washing the supper things until she judged that Joyce would be finished. And Reilof, wiping his hands at the end of his unaccustomed task, had said in that bland voice she was beginning to hate because it hid his feelings so effectively: 'That was thoughtful of you, Laura—do you intend to smooth my path as diligently when we're married?'

She had resented his cool assumption that she would accept him, even though she had more or less done so, but all she had said had been:

'No—I imagine you're perfectly able to do that for yourself. I thought it might have been awkward for Father.'

And he had laughed and murmured: 'Cut down to size for the second time today! And don't look so stricken, Laura, I dislike sympathy.'

'Wretch,' Laura reflected, 'ill-tempered, arrogant wretch—just let him wait until we're married!' Upon which satisfying resolution, not taking into account resentment or uncertainty or anything else, she fell sound asleep.

The astonishment on the Principal Nursing Officer's face when Laura presented herself at the office and gave in her notice was quite ludicrous.

Laura had seemed to her to be a safe bet for the rest of her working life, but she swallowed her surprise and asked in a coy voice which went ill with her stern visage, 'And who is the lucky man, Sister?'

'Doctor van Meerum, Miss Moore.'

It was difficult to know whether to be flattered or insulted by her superior's look of sheer disbelief. Her, 'You'll be living in Holland, then? Well, I must wish you every happiness and accept your resignation as from today, Sister Standish,' was uttered in a tone which implied that she considered the happiness rather doubtful. Laura conceded that she was probably right; any happiness which came her way she would have to fight for—excellent tooth and pretty pink nail.

There seemed little point in keeping her departure a secret, as the grapevine would get hold of it anyway, and rather than allow its sometimes inaccurate gossip to spread through the hospital, Laura told Ann while they were having their morning coffee together. The news spread like wildfire, and if its hearers were mystified by it, only the more indiscreet of them made reference to the fact that they had understood that it was Joyce who had become engaged to Doctor van Meerum. Those who did were hushed at once, for Laura was liked throughout the hospital and the good wishes she received were sincere. But in reply to the numerous questions as to when and where she would marry, where she would live, and most important of all, what she intended wearing for the wedding, she was forced to prevaricate, for she had only the haziest of ideas herself. Indeed, when she considered the matter, she wasn't sure if she had actually said that she would marry Reilof, and supposing, just supposing he had changed his mind?

He hadn't; she had taken it for granted that they would see each other again when she went home, but towards the end of the week he came to see her at St Anne's. The moment was hardly an auspicious one, for she was busily engaged in restraining one of the patients from removing the cannula from his arm; he had taken exception to the flask of blood hanging beside his bed and had made several attempts to tug the tubing free, each time restrained by Laura, who was outwardly composed but wishing heartily that her nurses would come back from their supper so that she could telephone George. The man was written up for more sedatives, but the difficulty was getting them ... she heard the step behind her with relief and said at once, still calmly, so that the other patients shouldn't be disturbed, 'George, do come and hang on to this arm while I get his injection.'

But the arm in its well-tailored sleeve which reached from behind her didn't belong to George; she would know that large well-kept hand anywhere. 'It's you!' she exclaimed idiotically.

'In person, and on this occasion arriving at the right time, I think.' He was beside her now and gave her a brief smile. 'Run along and get whatever it is he needs while I hold him—what is he?'

'A bad laceration of scalp with concussion—he really needs a special for a bit, but there's no one to spare until the night staff come on.'

She sped away, unpinning the D.D.A. key from her uniform as she went. It took only a few minutes to unlock the cupboard in her office, find the drug, check it and draw it up and then go quick-footed down the ward once more. Doctor van Meerum was standing just as she had left him, a firm hand on the patient, and he kept it there until she had given the injection and it had taken effect. Only when the man quietened and sank into unconsciousness once more did he relinquish his hold.

'No nurses?' he inquired.

'At supper—they'll be back any minute.'

'Surely a little rash to send everyone but yourself with such a patient on the ward?' His tone was mild, but she flushed.

'I have two first-year nurses on duty with me; it would have been most unfair to keep one back and then leave the other one by herself to cope while I gave the report.'

He said gravely, 'I stand corrected. Here they are now. Shall I stay for the moment? Just until you've given the report to the night nurses, that would allow your two to keep an eye on the other patients.'

She gave him a relieved glance. 'Oh, would you? It would be very kind—they're both very good, but it's their first ward and everything's strange. I'll be about ten minutes.'

She was as good as her word, and leaving the night

staff nurse and her junior as well as a third-year male student nurse to sit with the concussion case, she went down the ward once more, murmuring her goodnights to the patients as she went. Reilof had relinquished his post to the male nurse and was standing idly waiting for her, and turned without a word as she reached him. They left the ward together and started down the stone staircase.

'Supper?' he suggested.

Laura stopped to look up at him. 'That would be nice—are you staying here?'

'In London? Yes. There's a meeting I have to attend tomorrow. I flew over.'

She nodded. 'I see.' She searched his impassive face with anxious eyes. 'Have you heard from Joyce?'

There was no expression on his face at all, but his voice was bland. 'Should I have? No—what would be the point?'

Laura resumed her brisk trot down the stairs. 'Well—none, I suppose. I just thought ... well, that she might have explained ...'

'I think she gave all the explanation necessary in her letter. She's married now, Laura,' he gave her a mocking smile. 'Don't tell me that you're having ideas about her discovering that she has made a mistake and rushing back to me—you're wasting your time.'

They had reached the long corridor which would lead eventually to the back entrance of the Nurses' Home and Laura stopped. 'I go down here.'

'I'll wait for you at the front entrance. How long will you be? Ten minutes?'

She almost smiled, imagining what Joyce would have said if he had put that same question to her. Apparently her own appearance didn't matter all that much; it was a sobering reflection. All the same she used her ten minutes to good effect, showering and making up her face nicely and re-doing her hair into its neat topknot before putting on what Joyce called her middle-of-the-road Jaeger shirt-waister. Its soft silvery grey was kind to her mousiness and set off her charming figure to advantage. She caught up the grey flannel coat which matched it so exactly, tucked a rose-pink scarf into the dress's neck and sped towards the entrance, pleased that however sober her dress was, her shoes and handbag were high fashion, bought in a burst of extravagance only a few weeks previously.

Reilof was waiting, leaning against a wall talking to Mr Burnett. They both looked up as Laura crossed the vast expanse of floor, and came to meet her. Mr Burnett stayed talking for a few minutes before he wandered away and Reilof said briskly, 'Delightfully punctual—we'll get a taxi.'

They crossed the forecourt to the street and a passing taxi wheeled out of the traffic and stopped. 'The Baron of Beef,' instructed the doctor, and Laura, pleased that she knew what he was talking about, said: 'Oh, yes—Gutter Lane.'

'You've been there?' Reilof sounded very faintly bored and she wished suddenly that she hadn't come.

'No—but one of the chef's assistants was in the ward with a severed tendon.' She couldn't think of anything else to say after that and was thankful that their ride was a short one, and even more thankful to find that the restaurant was almost full of chattering people; at least the atmosphere was cheerful and would create the illusion of a pleasant meal *à deux*. She sat down with her usual composure, her busy mind mulling over topics of conversation which might serve to divert her companion.

She need not have bothered; once he had ordered their drinks and suggested that she might like to try the *pâté maison* and follow it with sole *au gratin*, while he himself decided on steak and kidney pudding with oysters to precede it, he sat back in his chair and said matter-of-factly: 'Now, let's discuss things in a businesslike fashion, shall we?'

Laura gave him a bleak look. Would they spend the rest of their lives being businesslike? she wondered unhappily. Perhaps with time, when he had got over Joyce, he would talk to her with the same warmth he had shown towards her sister and his eyes would smile instead of looking like black stone.

'By all means,' she agreed, and took a good sip of sherry to give her heart. It was an excellent sherry; she took another sip and felt a little better, relaxing in her chair, waiting for him to say whatever it was he wanted to be businesslike about. She had to wait a few minutes, for he said nothing at all, only looked at her in a thoughtful way as though he expected her to say something first. Well, she wasn't going to; she took a third sip of sherry and eyed him with faint belligerence.

He said surprisingly, 'You look nice—you always seem to wear slacks and blouses ...'

'Only because when I'm home I have the house to see to and do the cooking,' she pointed out tartly, and was instantly mollified by his,

'Well, you won't need to do that. I have an excellent housekeeper who will be only too glad to relieve you of both housework and cooking,' and then, as though he sensed that he hadn't said quite enough: 'Your cooking is excellent.'

'Thanks, but not on a par with this.' She indicated the pâté which had been set before her, and went on deliberately: 'Joyce didn't like cooking—how were you going to manage?'

His eyes were like black ice. 'I have just told you —I have an excellent housekeeper. Laura, will you oblige me by not talking about Joyce? There seems no point in doing so.'

She buttered a finger of toast and popped it into her mouth. 'Well, I won't if you don't want me to, but you can't just cut her out of your life like that.' She hesitated. 'Perhaps you can, though.'

He didn't answer her. 'Have you resigned your job?'

'Yes, I leave ...' she calculated quickly, 'in three weeks and a day.'

He nodded. 'Early July, that should suit us very well. We can have a quiet wedding and a short holiday before we return to Holland.'

She gave him a straight look. 'Aren't you being a little high-handed?' and had to wait for his answer while he sampled the wine the waiter had poured. When their glasses had been filled, he said: 'I beg your pardon, you've scarcely had time to make up your mind, have you?'

She replied with disarming honesty. 'Yes, I have, only you—you're taking everything for granted. If we're to make a success of it we have to start off with everything understood, don't we? I think,' she went on a little shyly, 'that we must be honest with each other, mustn't we? Like good friends.'

'I hope we shall be that, and you're quite right, of course. We must also undertake not to interfere in each other's lives.' He saw her bewildered look. 'That's to say, while we will, I hope, live together comfortably enough, there must be no question of encroaching upon each other's privacy.'

Just for a moment Laura quailed; the wish to put down her knife and fork and walk out of the restaurant was strong, but only for a moment. She loved this withdrawn, proud man sitting opposite her. Perhaps he would never love her, she strongly doubted it, but she might, in the course of time, win his affection. Anyway, what did life hold for her if she decided not to marry him after all? Nothing.

'A very good idea,' she agreed pleasantly. 'You will, of course, have to put me right as we go along. You were saying about the wedding ... is it to be from my home?'

'Why not?' he wanted to know coolly. 'I'll bring

the car over and we can go somewhere quiet—the West Country perhaps.'

'That would be nice. Just exactly where do you live, Reilof?'

'Between Hilversum and Baarn in a very pleasant part of the country. There are woods around and villages tucked well away from the roads. My home is almost exactly between the two towns, very convenient, as I have beds in Hilversum hospital and consulting rooms in both places. Patients occasionally come to the house, too. I have a partner, a good deal younger than myself—Jan van Nijhof.'

Laura sat silent while the waiter served her sole, and only when they had started to eat again did she ask him: 'And family?'

'A married sister in den Haag, two younger brothers—one has a practice in Toronto, the other is working for his fellowship at Leiden. My mother is dead and my father lives in Loenen, a small place quite close to Hilversum. He retired several years ago, although he occasionally does some lecturing.'

'All doctors,' commented Laura, very much struck.

'Every man jack of us, and my sister is married to an orthopaedic surgeon.' He smiled so nicely at her that she was emboldened to ask, 'Did they know that you were going to get married?'

'I mentioned the possibility, no more.'

She heaved a sigh of relief. 'Oh, good.' She added in a muddled fashion, 'I mean they won't know it's me instead of Joyce.'

Presumably he understood her, for he agreed

blandly before asking her what she would like for a sweet; quite obviously he wasn't going to discuss his feelings on the subject. She ate the delicious sorbet set before her with no more pleasure than if it had been the prunes and custard so often offered in the hospital canteen, while she talked with determined cheerfulness about the weather, the prospect of a warm summer, the little dog he had rescued and other safe but rather dull topics. Her companion, replying to her remarks with unfailing politeness, demonstrated to her quite clearly that he was thinking about other things. They got up to go finally, still exchanging platitudes, and at the hospital entrance she broke off her muddled thanks for her dinner to say: 'It won't do, you know—you're bored stiff with me, aren't you, and hating every minute. We'd better stop now before it's too late ...'

His sudden grip on her arm made her wince. 'Laura, I'm sorry. If I have appeared bored, believe me that wasn't the case; if I've been a poor companion, I apologise, but I have to make a fresh start and you can help me—you're helping me already, just by being you; quiet and undemanding, allowing me my ill humour and lack of interest. If you will have patience just for a little while ...' He half smiled. 'I'm a poor bargain, aren't I? But you see, it's rather like waking up from a beautiful dream and getting used to reality again. Very likely I shall find reality far better than the dream, but I have to forget the dream first.' He loosed his hold on her arm and took her hands in his. 'Do you know, I

74

don't believe that I could have said that to anyone else?'

He bent suddenly and kissed her gently, and she stood looking up at him, smiling uncertainly. She didn't know whether to laugh or cry, and when he observed, 'I have always thought of you as a plain girl, but I was mistaken. When you smile you're quite pretty,' she had no words with which to meet his remark, so she wished him goodnight and went up to her room, to sit before her dressing-table mirror and stare at her face.

Presently she got up and started to get ready for bed. 'He must have been looking at me in a poor light,' she remarked to the room at large.

He came, to her surprise, the following day, and put his head round the office door while she was sitting at her desk writing up the charts.

'You're off at five o'clock?' he wanted to know; a rhetorical question, since he already knew, but Laura said cheerfully that yes, she was, and why?

'If you're not too tired, would it be a good idea to go to your home and have a word with the local parson?'

'Of course, why not?' Her placid face showed nothing of the excitement tearing around inside her. She added prosaically: 'I shall probably be a little late—ops day, you know.'

Reilof went away after a few minutes, leaving her to jumble up the charts in a hopeless manner while she tried to look into her future. A quiet wedding, he had said, and then a brief holiday—could one call it a honeymoon? She thought not—she would have to think about clothes, it was a cheering thought to brighten her other, gloomier ones.

It said much for her good sense that she gave her usual careful report to Pat when she came on duty, personal thoughts damped down.

She wore the Jaeger dress again, for the evening, though bright, was cool, and by dint of hurrying she managed to reach the hospital entrance as it was striking six o'clock. It was as she was hurrying down the corridors that she recollected that Reilof hadn't got the car with him—they would have to go by train and at this time of the day it would be packed. But as she reached the door she saw Reilof leaning against the bonnet of an old Morris which she recognized as belonging to George.

When she reached it she exclaimed, 'Hullo, how on earth did you get George to lend you his car? He never lends it ...'

'There's an exception to every rule,' he remarked easily. 'He swears it goes like a bomb, but I'm not so sure—as long as it gets us there and back again.' He opened the door for her and then went round to sit beside her. 'This will teach me not to come over without a car.'

'Then why did you?'

They were edging into the evening traffic. 'I hadn't a great deal of time and I wanted to see you, Laura.'

She couldn't think of anything else to say but 'Oh,' and then sat silent until at length the traffic thinned a little as they reached London's outskirts. Only then she asked, 'Why?'

It was surprising what speed he was getting out of the elderly car. 'I wanted to be certain—not of myself, but of you; to know that you really meant what you had said; to get our plans made and settled.'

Laura could understand that; he had to forget Joyce, hadn't he? as quickly as he could, and he was going the right way about it, although it must be a painful experience. She suspected that he was a man of determination when it was needed and she was sure that once they were married he would treat her with consideration, albeit perhaps with indifference. But he certainly wouldn't throw Joyce in her teeth, and would never let her feel that she was second choice. She paused in her reflections to say: 'If you turn off left at the next crossroads there's a short cut ...'

Presently he began to talk—about nothing in particular it was true, but it was agreeable to find that they had quite a lot in common, and even though he hardly noticed her as a girl they were getting on far better than she had imagined. By the time they reached her home she was beginning to feel completely at home with him, and fancied that he too felt the same. All to the good, she told herself as she got out of the car, since they'd chosen to share their life together.

The evening passed satisfactorily; her father seemed to have accepted the situation without much trouble, and Uncle Wim behaved as though the pair of them had intended to marry all along. They talked for a bit, the four of them, and then Laura took Reilof down the road to the rectory, where the Rector, a dear, dreamy man with a frightful memory, discussed their wedding with evident pleasure, digressing a good deal to inquire after Joyce, and even breaking off in the middle of a sentence to say: 'I rather thought that our little Joyce had been thinking of marrying you, Doctor van Meerum, which just shows how mistaken one can be. She showed me a magnificent ring one day, I remember, but she refused to tell me who had given it to her—now I realise that it was this rich young man from America. I hope the dear child is very happy—such a pity that they were unable to marry here. I daresay that you've heard from her?'

The doctor said gravely that no, he hadn't, and reminded the Rector that he hadn't told them if ten o'clock in the morning would be too early an hour at which to be married.

'Certainly not—and it's to be a quiet wedding, that seems to me to be an excellent choice. Of course Laura is well known in the village and popular, too, but she would hardly want to wear white satin and orange blossom.' He smiled with kindly tactlessness at her. 'I remember when you were christened, my dear—almost thirty years ago.'

Laura choked and caught Reilof's eye and saw the gleam in it before managing to say, 'I've not had time to think what I shall wear, but I'm sure it won't be white satin. May we settle for ten o'clock then, Mr Lamb? And now we really must go; I'm on duty in the morning, you know.'

As they walked back Reilof observed: 'It would serve everyone right if you were to turn up in bridal finery and a dozen bridesmaids behind you.' He looked down at her thoughtfully, and she thought that he was really seeing her. 'You don't look as old as you are,' he told her kindly, a remark which left her seething, although she thanked him in a colourless voice and bit back the retort ready on her tongue, while a resolve, a little vague as yet, took shape in the back of her head that one day he should eat his words.

The rest of the evening passed pleasantly enough. No one, meeting the doctor for the first time, would have guessed, even remotely, that he was suffering from a broken heart. His manners were delightful, he entered into the conversation readily, and gave no indication of his true feelings, and only when Uncle Wim deliberately introduced Joyce into their talk did Laura see the little muscle twitching at the corner of his mouth and his face assume the bland expression she so much disliked.

All the same, their return journey was cheerful enough, although she would have been happier if he had shown more interest in their wedding. He saw her to the Nurses' Home, assured her that he would be seeing her again before long and wished her good-night, adding: 'I have a ring for you, I must remember to give it to you the next time we meet.'

A more casual way of becoming engaged she had

yet to discover. She fumed her way to bed, alternately positive that she wouldn't marry such a wretchedly unfeeling man, and just as sure that she would make him such a good wife that he would forget Joyce completely.

CHAPTER FIVE

THE next three weeks passed quickly. Laura embarked on a shopping expedition, using up a good deal of the money she had saved during the last few years; refusing the good-natured help of her friends, she spent her free time combing the shops for exactly what she wanted, pretty clothes which would detract from the plainness of her face. She chose a beautifully cut dress and jacket for her wedding in a rich clotted cream crêpe with a little turban hat of the same colour patterned with green and turquoise and ruby red; this last as a concession to the ring Reilof had given her—the ring Joyce had refused to wear because it was old-fashioned. Laura loved it; its three rubies were set in an oblong of diamonds and mounted on gold, and it had fitted her finger exactly. Childishly she had taken that as a good omen.

She had bought shoes and handbag to go with her wedding outfit too, and then laid out the rest of her money on a dress or two, more shoes and sandals and all the undies she could afford. It was after she had spent all her money that she recollected that her evening dresses were out of date and few in number; perhaps Reilof didn't go out much in the evening, but it would be awful to find that he did and she had nothing to wear. She was pondering the problem when it was solved for her by the unexpected cheque which her father sent her, and she spent the whole of it on two long dresses, one a pale pink chiffon with a tiny bodice and a floating cape and the other brown, the colour of her eyes, with little cape sleeves trimmed with lace, its low neckline trimmed with lace too.

Satisfied at last with her purchases, she invited her friends to view her new wardrobe and was delighted when they presented her with a gift—a suitcase, not leather, it was true, but smart and good-looking all the same. She packed her new finery into it feeling that at least she wouldn't put Reilof to shame with shabby possessions, and left St Anne's for the last time.

Most of the odds and ends and her other clothes had already been sent home, and Reilof was to pick her up on his way from Holland. He was waiting for her as she went through the main door, a handful of her closest friends with her. And this time there was no Aston Martin but a silver-grey Rolls-Royce drawn up in the forecourt. Laura hesitated for a moment, feeling suddenly uncertain, but he came to meet her and in the burst of talk from her companions she forgot the uncertainty and felt only excitement. All the same she had lost her tongue, and it was only when she had said her final goodbyes and had been ushered into the car and Reilof was beside her that she said: 'How super being met by a Rolls ...'

He smiled a little. 'It seemed a more suitable car

to the occasion than the Aston Martin.'

'Well, yes—I suppose so, but aren't you a bit nervous of driving it?'

He sounded amused. 'Er—no, not in the least. I've been driving one for some years now.'

She turned a surprised face to him. 'It's not yours?'

'Yes, it is. You sound disapproving, Laura.'

'Well, I don't mean to be.' She hesitated, watching him steer the big car through the traffic. 'I know it's not my business and I don't mean to pry, but are you very successful?'

'If by that carefully wrapped up question you want to know if I can afford to run a Rolls, yes, I can. And it is your business.'

Laura frowned. 'I didn't wrap up the question,' she pointed out rather coldly, 'how very horrid of you to say so. I'm sure I don't wish to know anything you don't choose to tell me.' She glared out of the window, feeling remarkably put out, and then looked at him as his hand covered hers for a moment.

'It's quite my fault,' he observed mildly. 'I've never discussed anything with you, have I? We've not had much time, but I'll tell you anything you want to know while we're on holiday. And there's a letter from my father in the pocket beside you— take it out and read it.'

She did as she was told, carefully scrutinising the writing on the envelope before she opened it; it was large and flowing and somehow it reassured her. The letter within wasn't all that long, but it warmed her heart. Reilof's father must be a dear. She didn't know if he had known about Joyce, but even if he had, there was no sign of it in his letter. It welcomed her into the family with a warmth she hadn't expected, and the writer expressed the hope that they would meet and become friends very soon: 'For I am sure that Reilof's wife will be as dear to me as to him,' it ended. She folded it carefully and put it back in its envelope, feeling almost physical hurt at the words, because of course Reilof's father would imagine her to be a much loved bride. He couldn't know about Joyce ...

Reilof's voice cut across her reflections. 'Father knows about Joyce. I've explained the whole to him, for of course I had described her to him and he would have been surprised ...'

Laura flushed brightly, went pale and then to her horror felt the tears welling up into her throat. Nothing she could do would stop them, they trickled down her cheeks and she didn't dare wipe them away, for he might turn and see what she was doing. Better to sit quite still.

Too still, though, for he glanced briefly at her, made a small sound which could have meant anything, and pulled the car into the side of the suburban road along which they were driving.

He stared at her wet cheeks for a few seconds. 'Something I've said?' he asked gently. 'You don't feel well?'

Her charming bosom heaved as she found her voice, rather watery but almost steady. 'I feel very well. Of course your father would be surprised; he expected a lovely golden-haired young girl, didn't he? And all he'll get is me, nudging thirty and as p-plain as a p-pikestaff. But you needn't have told me—do you really think I don't know?'

She felt his arm across her shoulders, pulling her comfortably close.

'Oh, my dear girl, what a clumsy wretch I am, and I had no thought of hurting you—and Father won't be surprised. I told him about you, but I mentioned neither your looks nor your age, although why that should matter I can't imagine.'

'It matters very much,' she assured him rather peevishly, 'and if you were a woman you'd understand.' She sat up straight and blew her nose and managed to smile. 'Oh dear, I don't know why I had to behave like a fool. I'm sorry.'

'Wedding nerves,' he observed comfortably. 'I believe all brides are supposed to have them.'

Joyce hadn't. Perhaps if you were going to marry a man you loved so much that you were prepared to throw over another man with no compunction at all, you were beyond nerves. Laura said with a certainty she didn't feel: 'Yes, I expect that's it, for I'm not usually so silly. I'll not do it again.'

His smile was kind. 'Then you will be a very exceptional wife. Esme—we married when she was eighteen—was very nervous at our wedding. It was rather a grand one—she had that sort of mother.'

'What was she like? Or would you rather not talk about her?'

'I was twenty-four when we married and she died eleven years ago of leukaemia.'

'Reilof, I'm sorry, how terrible for you. Perhaps you'd rather not tell me . . .'

He had started the car again and they were approaching the more open Essex countryside. He said slowly: 'It's a long time ago now, and months before she died I knew that I'd married the wrong girl. She hated my work—hospitals, going out at all hours of the day and night, coming home late and leaving early—poor Esme, she was very young. I believe that she had no idea of the life she would lead as a doctor's wife.'

He was silent for a few moments and then went on quietly: 'I suppose we were happy for about six months, and then in a year or less I began to suspect that she was ill—she never knew. I took a partner and cut my work to a minimum so that she could enjoy the kind of life she wanted; dining out, dancing, theatres, holidays in the south of France. Shortly after she died my partner went abroad and I was on my own for a few years, but the practice got large and I began to lecture as well. I took a partner last year, Jan van Mijhof, he's younger than I, a very good sort too and a first-rate doctor. He's not married and lives close by. I should warn you that I am a busy man, Laura.'

'Well, I shall have plenty to occupy me—I shall have to learn Dutch, shan't I?' She thought for a moment. 'There's the little dog, too—I can take him for walks. What do you call him?'

'Lucky. Oh, yes, he likes his exercise and so does Hovis, my other dog. The country round about the house is very pretty, I think you'll like it.' He glanced at her. 'Do you ride?'

'I haven't done for years. I daresay I'd be all right on a very staid kind of horse.'

He laughed. 'Well, we'll have to see about that.'

She asked rather wistfully, 'I suppose you don't want any help in the surgery?'

'Er—no. Later on perhaps. I have a surgery nurse and a secretary, and if either of them should be ill I might be glad of your offer.'

His voice sounded friendly enough, but she could hear a note of reserve; he didn't want her to have anything to do with his work; she would have to remember that. She started to talk about something else and kept the conversation to trivialities until they reached her home.

An hour later, in the kitchen getting supper, Laura found it difficult to believe that she was actually getting married the next day; her father and Uncle Wim had been delighted to see her, but their interest in the forthcoming wedding was only mild. Of course they were delighted that she was to be the bride, but she suspected that they were equally delighted that it was to be such a very quiet affair, necessitating no unnecessary dressing up and no fuss and bother with guests, wedding breakfasts, and the like. And as for Reilof, once he had taken their things up to their rooms, he had settled down with the two older men, to an absorbing discussion of some medical matter. Even Mrs Whittaker, who would have been an interested and highly satisfactory audience, was at home nursing her brood of children through the measles.

It was left to Mittens to be Laura's confidante, and she only pretended interest while she waited for her supper. Laura, longing to discuss the most important event in her life so far, sighed, and then chided herself for giving way to self-pity. She had made her bed and she was going to lie in it, she assured Mittens as she offered the little cat her evening saucer of milk.

'And what exactly do you mean by that?' asked Reilof from the door, and when she turned to look at him he wasn't smiling.

'Nothing,' she told him swiftly. 'Have you come to see if supper's ready?'

He seemed content to let his question go unanswered. 'Your father has opened a bottle of champagne and he wants you to join us.' He glanced round the kitchen in a vague way. 'Is there anything I can do?'

She told him no and went with him to her father's study and smiled at the gentlemen when they toasted her, laughed obligingly at Uncle Wim's gentle little jokes about weddings in general and hers in particular, and then went back to the kitchen to dish up.

As the evening progressed she found that she had no feelings at all about the next morning's ceremony, only a kind of hazy acceptance of it; the haziness was probably due to the champagne. Just after ten o'clock she wished the three men good night and went up to her room, where she laid her wedding clothes ready, washed her hair, did her nails and jumped into bed, to fall immediately, contrary to her expectations, into a refreshing sleep disturbed only by her alarm clock sounding off seven o'clock the next morning.

Not quite five hours later she was in her bedroom again, making ready to leave with Reilof. The wedding had been a surprisingly cheerful affair, for despite the lack of guests the church had been filled to capacity by those people in the village who had known her for most of her life. Indeed, she had been astonished when she and her father, after walking the short distance from her home to the church, had been greeted by so many smiling expectant faces, all staring over their shoulders to get a first glimpse of her. She faltered a little, but then she saw Reilof waiting for her, the only person in the church not looking at her. He could have least shown a little interest, she fumed silently as she and her father started down the aisle, and then her ill-feeling vanished, because as she reached his side he looked down at her, not smiling but kind and reassuring, and she felt absurdly happy despite the doubtful future.

She got out of her wedding outfit and packed it carefully before getting into the cotton shirtwaister —a pretty garment patterned in summer flowers on a silvery grey ground—did her face and hair and stood wondering what to do with the elegant little spray of orange-blossom, roses and orchids which Reilof had given her before he had left for the church that morning. It seemed pointless to keep it, for it had been given with a casually friendly, 'Brides always have flowers—I don't see why you should be the exception,' which had robbed the gift of any sentiment, but all the same she wrapped it tenderly in a scrap of tissue paper and slipped it into her overnight bag before going downstairs to inform her three companions that she was ready.

They were sitting around in the study, talking easily just as though the day were the same as any other. Reilof, she saw at once, had changed the beautifully-cut grey suit he had worn in church for an equally well-cut tweed jacket and cavalry twill trousers; the ring she had given him during the ceremony caught her eye, and without knowing that she did it, she touched her own wedding ring beneath the rubies of her engagement ring.

Reilof looked up then and saw her standing in the doorway and got to his feet, saying easily: 'Ah, here she is—I'll go and get the car and fetch the bags, shall I, while you say goodbye.'

It was a splendid summer's day and the Rolls ate up the miles. For the first few of them Laura had nothing to say, but presently, anxious to break the silence, she asked: 'You don't think Uncle Wim will mind staying another week with Father? I believe he meant to go back to Holland several weeks ago . . .'

Reilof swung the car away from Chelmsford,

taking a country road which would bring them out on to the London road beyond Ongar. 'I'm sure he doesn't mind at all, and probably when we go back for him in a week's time he'll find some excuse for staying even longer.' He added to surprise her, 'You looked very nice this morning, Laura, and that's a pretty dress you're wearing.'

She could think of nothing to say but a murmured thank-you, and presently, to fill the silence, inquired which way they would go.

'The ring road—we can pick up the motorway at Chertsey, it will take us as far as Cadnam Corner.'

'Oh—exactly where are we going?'

'Heavens, did I not tell you? I've booked rooms at Corfe Castle. Do you know it?'

'I've been there once or twice, but never to stay. I liked it.'

'It won't be very quiet at this time of year, I'm afraid, but I thought we might drive out each day and go where inclination takes us. But if you don't like the idea, do say so and we'll try something else.'

'But I do like it,' she said positively, 'and I love exploring.'

The journey passed pleasantly enough, indeed, Laura was hard put to it to remember that she was actually married to the man beside her. It seemed more as though they were two friends out for the day, bent on entertaining each other. Only when they reached Corfe Castle and entered the picturesque old hotel in its little square was the fact of her married status brought home to her when she was

addressed as Madam and heard Reilof saying that
Mrs van Meerum would like to go to her room as
soon as someone could be found to carry up her
luggage.

She followed the porter upstairs to the first land-
ing, where she discovered that they were to have two
adjoining rooms at the back of the hotel. Very comfortable they were too, each with a bathroom and
furnished with old-fashioned comfort. There was no
sign of Reilof, so she unpacked her case, tidied her
hair, saw to her face and wandered out on to the
small balcony, where he presently joined her. It
might have been the balcony scene from *Private
Lives*; only their conversation held no hint of
romance, for he asked at once if she was hungry and
if so, would it not be a good idea for them to dine
early and then take a stroll through the little town.
'I'll be back in fifteen minutes,' he suggested as he
strolled away to his own room.

She changed her dress, more to please herself than
for any other reason; since she had some pretty
clothes she might as well wear them, and the round-
necked, short-sleeved silk jersey dress in a pleasing
shade of honey was certainly pretty. But if Reilof
noticed it, he forbore from saying so, merely com-
mending her on her promptitude as they went downstairs to the dining room where they had a leisurely
meal at a small table in the window, a circumstance
which Laura considered fortunate, for there was
plenty to see in the square and it made a happy
source of conversation. The dining room was almost

full, but no one, she decided, would have any idea that they were newly married.

Indeed, their manner was more that of a couple who had been man and wife for some years, who, while enjoying each other's company, weren't excited by it. It was on the tip of her tongue to make some joking remark about it, but perhaps it would be as well to wait until they were on their own, for he might not find it amusing. It was disconcerting when he remarked: 'We must be the most untypical newly married couple ever heard of.' He smiled with sudden charm. 'Perhaps we should have gone to one of those enormous anonymous hotels where they hold dinner dances every night and you're known by your room number.'

She doubted very much if he had ever been to such a place, but she had followed his train of thought easily enough. 'No,' she declared firmly, 'it's quiet here and we have to get to know each other—I mean, you never really get to know anyone if you just go out to dinners and dances and theatres with them, do you?'

He agreed gravely and asked quietly, 'You're not regretting our marriage, Laura?'

She shook her head. 'No, but then I haven't got used to it yet, though I can't think of any reason why I should regret it, you know. I had a month in which to think about it and I'm not an impulsive girl.'

He raised his brows. 'Not in general, I think, but surely you were a little impulsive when you agreed to marry me?'

She went pink, although she poured his coffee with a steady hand and handed him the cup. 'You were impulsive to suggest it,' she pointed out. 'I daresay it's a good thing to do something on the spur of the moment now and again.' She sugared her coffee. 'There are a great many questions I should like to ask you during the next few days, so I hope you won't mind answering them.'

'I'll do my best, but shall we leave them until to-morrow? It's a delightful evening, we might walk round the town if you would like that.'

And it had been very pleasant, Laura decided as she got ready for bed. Strolling along, peering into the small shop windows, discussing where they should go, wandering round the church, reading the memorial tablets on its walls and then back to the hotel for a drink before bed. She yawned hugely, deliberately dwelling on the trivialities of the day; it hadn't been like a wedding day at all, but she hadn't expected that it would be, and she had promised herself that she wouldn't dwell on her love for Reilof but be thankful for what she had got. Not much, she decided sleepily, but the thin end of the wedge, perhaps? Or did she mean half a loaf was better than no bread at all? She wasn't sure, and she was too sleepy to decide.

Life seemed normal again after a sound night's sleep, and nothing could have been more prosaic than Reilof's manner at breakfast. They spent their day in Salisbury because Laura had expressed a

wish to see the cathedral again, lunched at the Rose
and Crown and then made their way back to Corfe
Castle, keeping to the country roads and stopping
for tea at a little cottage run by an old lady, very
spry despite her grey hair, who served them with
strong tea in a brown pot, scones of her own baking
and a great dish of clotted cream and strawberry
jam besides. Laura made a good tea, quite at ease
now with Reilof after a day's undemanding conversation with him. They hadn't talked much of his
home, although he had given her snippets of information about Holland and the way of life there.
Very much the same as in England, she had considered, and wished that he would tell her more
about himself and his family—still, there would be
all the time in the world to do that when they got
back. She polished off the last of the scones, bade the
old lady a cheerful goodbye and accompanied
Reilof back to the car, where he invited her to get
into the driving seat and try her hand.

'I don't dare,' she protested vigorously. 'Supposing I should smash it up—it's a Rolls ...'

'You haven't smashed a car up yet, have you?' he
wanted to know calmly. 'I can see no reason why you
should do so now. Besides, I shan't let you.'

She was nervous at first, but presently she forgot
she was driving a wildly expensive car which wasn't
hers and began to enjoy herself. Only when they re-
joined the main road once more did Reilof take over
again, assuring her that she drove very well and that
once they were back in Holland she should have a

car of her own. 'Nothing too large, though.'

'But you've got two cars already,' she pointed out.

'It will be best for you to have your own, all the same,' he told her reasonably, and began to talk about something else.

They went out each day, sometimes merely pottering through the lanes around the town, sometimes going farther afield, and although Laura still felt a slight constraint between them, she was content that they enjoyed each other's company well enough, and as she pointed out to herself in the privacy of her room, they were all day and every day together now, and once they were in Holland they would see far less of each other. If they could get through the week without falling out or getting on each other's nerves, she felt that it augured well for the future.

It was the day before they were due to return that they visited the Blue Pool. They had been recommended to visit it by several people at the hotel, but somehow there had always been other places to see and other things to do, but now, after spending the morning at Lulworth Cove, already over-full of holidaymakers, they decided to find it on their way back to the hotel. They took the narrow road over the hills that wound its way in and out of hamlets, apparently going nowhere. The day had been fine and now in the afternoon it was pleasantly cool as they drove slowly down the narrow lane for the last mile or so of their journey, and even then they weren't quite there, for there was a narrow, half-hidden track to negotiate before they found themselves in a large clearing with the entrance to the Blue Pool at one side of it.

They parked the car and went through the gates into the grounds surrounding the pool, and at first Laura thought it all a bit overrated; there were some splendid trees and shrubs, true enough, but there was no sign of a pool ... they saw it unexpectedly, lying below them, a deep circle of bright blue ringed by a narrow strip of sand and dense shrubs, intersected by a great many narrow paths.

'How absolutely super,' exclaimed Laura, craning her neck to see through the bushes, 'and what a heavenly blue!'

'The special clay bed,' Reilof informed her, 'but don't ask me more than that, because I don't know. It is rather splendid.' He took her hand and her heart, taken unawares, turned over. 'There's a path, shall we explore a little?'

They wandered slowly round the water, catching glimpses of it below them, and as they went they discovered a bench perched high on a bank, and sat down. For some reason there were very few people about, and from where they sat they could hear the distant laughter and cries of some children on the other side of the pool, and all around them the birds singing. It was peaceful as well as beautiful.

'If ever I wanted to run away from anything,' mused Laura out loud, 'and hide, I think I should come here.'

Reilof looked at her sharply. 'Why do you say that?'

'No reason really, just a feeling. I don't usually run away from anything and I can't imagine having a reason—it would have to be something quite dreadful.' She smiled at him. 'We go back tomorrow, you know, and I still don't know very much about your home.'

'It will be *our* home now,' he observed, and she heard the bitterness in his voice and winced at it. She had tried very hard during the last few days to get to know him better and she believed that they had become friends, but she didn't know his deepest feelings. He would still be in love with Joyce, she was sure of that, but that was to be expected. She would have to have patience and in the meantime play the colourless part he had offered her.

She sighed soundlessly and then said cheerfully: 'I'd love a cup of tea—could we try that tea-room we passed as we came in, do you think?'

Forty-eight hours later, sitting beside Reilof once more and with Uncle Wim in the back seat as they drove up to Harwich to catch the ferry to Holland, she decided that on the whole their first week together had gone well. At least they were quite at ease with each other now, and when her godfather had asked her, 'Are you happy, Laura?' she had been able to say yes and mean it. She had reservations about the future, of course, but they could be faced later on.

CHAPTER SIX

IT was most unfortunate that by the time they reached Harwich, the weather had changed very much for the worse; clouds which had been hovering on the horizon all day suddenly massed themselves together, blown by a freak gale, bringing not only rain with it, but thunder and lightning as well. Laura didn't like storms, and she paled a little with each flash and moved, almost without knowing it, nearer Reilof, so that when they went on board she sighed with relief and went straight to her cabin before joining her companions in the bar.

'Tonic water?' suggested Reilof with a sidelong glance at her pale face, and when they had finished their drinks and Uncle Wim had voiced his intention to go to his cabin without delay, Reilof suggested that they might go on deck for a little while. The rain had ceased by now and the storm was a mere muttering in the distance, and only the wind howled and sighed around them. Laura, her hair in a splendid tangle, clung to a nice solid rail and looked with loathing at the heaving water below.

'It's going to be rough,' she observed in a hollow voice, and was irritated by her companion's cheerful, 'Oh, I imagine so—there's a gale force wind.' He dismissed this disquieting news carelessly and went on, 'Take a look behind you, Laura; you won't be seeing England again for a little while.'

She didn't care if she never saw it again. She said in a carefully controlled voice, 'I'm going to be sick,' and Reilof, who had never been sick in his life, gave her a startled look, said: 'My God, so you are,' and proceeded to deal with the situation with a calm matter-of-factness which, if she hadn't been feeling quite so ghastly, would have earned Laura's approbation. As it was, she was only too thankful to have someone there to hold her head, and presently, when the worst was over, to help her down to her cabin. Here she made a great effort to pull herself together, but Reilof took no notice at all of her rather half-hearted protestations that she was feeling fine, but laid her out on her bunk, took off her shoes, covered her with a blanket, wiped her face with a damp towel and rang for the stewardess. Laura didn't see him go, for the cabin was revolving and dipping in a most alarming manner and she had shut her eyes; when she opened them again it was the kindly face of the stewardess which she saw hovering above her.

'Yer 'usband says yer ter 'ave this, Mrs van Meerum,' she said in a cheerful cockney voice, 'a nice drop o' brandy.'

'Ugh,' said Laura, drank it obediently and mumbled that she would be sick again at any moment, then went soundly to sleep.

She slept until shortly before they landed and woke to a still tossing ship which miraculously didn't matter any more, although she felt very hollow. But fortified by the tea and toast the stewardess had brought, she made shift to make herself presentable, so that when Reilof came to fetch her she looked much as usual, although still wan, in sharp contrast to his own elegant appearance, for he had the look of a man who had slept all night and who had, moreover, the time to spare in which to make a leisurely toilet.

That he had remained awake for the greater part of the night and had visited her half a dozen times at least during it was something she didn't even guess at. During the whole of her life she had never been cosseted by her parents even though they had loved her; the cosseting had all been for Joyce and she had long ago become used to it, so that now it never entered her head that anyone, and certainly not Reilof, should concern themselves about her. She wished him good morning in a composed manner, begged his pardon for making a nuisance of herself on the previous evening, and accompanied him on deck where her godfather was waiting. He, it turned out, had slept like a log and had never felt better. The two men, thought Laura, standing between them, looked quite disgustingly healthy, which put her at a disadvantage, although neither of them mentioned her seasickness, merely hoping that she felt well before they embarked on a discussion as to the best road to take when they disembarked.

The boat was full and most of the passengers were already crowding into the saloon, anxious to rejoin their cars on the car deck, but Reilof seemed unaware of this; he leaned against the ship's rail, one arm flung carelessly across Laura's shoulders while he argued lazily with Uncle Wim, and pausing now and then to point out something of interest to her as the ferry crept to its berth at the quayside. Only then, when the first rush of passengers had subsided, did he usher his companions back to the car.

One of the last off, once they had cleared the little town he shot the Rolls ahead, and when they joined the motorway a few miles further on he outstripped everything ahead of them. 'It will be a dull trip,' he warned Laura, 'motorway all the way, but it's quick and your godfather is anxious to get home—he lives quite close to us. We'll drop him off first.' He glanced at her. 'Once we're through Rotterdam we'll stop for coffee.' He added with a faint smile, 'I daresay you're feeling a little empty.'

Laura admitted to hunger. 'But don't stop on my account,' she begged him, 'if Uncle Wim wants to get home...' She added, 'Is it far?'

'About sixty miles—no distance. We shall be home in time for a very late breakfast. All the same, we'll stop.'

He drew up before a pleasant-looking road house just off the motorway very shortly after, and although it was still early the coffee when it came was hot and fragrant and creamy. Laura had two cups and a *kaas broodje* besides and got back into the car feeling almost her own self again, so that she was able to obey her godfather's gentle demands to look at first one landmark, then another. The motorway might be dull, but the flat country around them made it possible to get a wide view of it, as well as getting a distant glimpse of the various towns and villages they skirted. They bypassed Utrecht, the doctor barely slackening speed, and took a side road to Baarn; the country was prettier here and wooded, and there were large villas tucked away almost out of sight of the road. Laura craned her neck in her efforts to see everything, and when her godfather warned her that they would be passing the royal palace in only a few moments, she begged Reilof to slow down just a little. 'Only for a moment,' she pleaded, 'just so that I can see it.'

He laughed and did as she asked, pointing out at the same time that as they lived quite close by, she would be able to see it as often as she wished in the future.

'Oh, are we almost there?' she wanted to know, and felt a small thrill of excitement and apprehension. Supposing the house was awful—it might even be a flat; she had never thought of asking and now it was too late. And supposing the housekeeper he had told her about didn't like her, or she didn't like the housekeeper? What if none of his friends liked her —worse still, his family? Her gloomy thoughts were brought to a halt by Reilof's quiet: 'There's the palace.'

He had slowed the car's splendid rush only momentarily, and a moment later he had put on speed again and presently, at a busy crossroads, had taken the left-hand fork to stop within a minute or two to slide the car gently into a tree-lined avenue of pleasant houses, each standing in its own garden. Halfway down he turned again, this time through a white-painted gateway, and drew up before a white-walled villa with a thatched roof: Doctor van Pette's house. Its door was instantly opened by an elderly, gaunt woman, who bustled out, bursting into speech as she came. The two men greeted her like an old friend, and Reilof said: 'This is Miekje, your godfather's housekeeper—she rules him with a rod of iron and he loves it. We have been asked to go in, but I think we should go straight home now. Wait there while I take the luggage in.'

Laura bade her godfather goodbye, promised to see him at the first opportunity, and sat quietly while his bags were taken indoors and Reilof made his own goodbyes before getting in beside her once more.

'He's tired,' he said abruptly. 'I've sent him straight to bed—a day's rest won't do him any harm.'

'He's not ill?' she asked sharply.

'No—but he's had a couple of coronaries, you know, and he's well into his seventies.' He smiled at her. 'I have the greatest dislike of my patients taking risks.'

'Oh, he's your patient—I should have guessed that, shouldn't I?'

They were back on the main road again; a magnificent one, lined with great trees backed by woods through which she caught an occasional glimpse of a house. 'Where are we now?' she wanted to know.

'Halfway between Baarn and Hilversum.' He slowed to cross the road and go through an open gate way between tall brick pillars, and she said: 'Is this it?' in such a scared voice that he said instantly, 'There's no need for you to worry, Laura.'

The drive was short, bordered by shrubs and ornamental trees, and beyond its curve the house came into view.

'Well, I never!' exclaimed Laura with a surprise which brought the doctor to an abrupt halt.

'You don't like it?' he asked quietly.

She turned to stare up at him. 'Like it?' she whispered. 'Like it? It's magnificent. I don't know what I expected and you didn't tell me ... it's a bit scaring, actually.'

'Oh, never that, my dear girl—it's old and rambling at the back, and I suppose it's a little on the large side, but it's never scared anyone in its long life.'

He spoke lightly, laughing at her, and she made haste to explain: 'Not the house—it's just that I'm going to live in it, and it's rather grand.' She added with faint annoyance, 'You could have told me!'

'I never thought about it,' he answered her suavely, and she knew, just as though he had told her in so many words, that he hadn't wanted to; probably he had planned to tell Joyce, describing to her every stick and stone lovingly ...

For something to say, she asked: 'It's old—eighteenth century?'

'Yes—the first half. Anyone who had any money at all then built their houses in some pleasant country spot not too far from Amsterdam—twenty miles or so—even in those days it wasn't a great distance.'

He had stopped the car on the wide gravel sweep before the great door, and while he was getting out she had another good look. The house was large, with a flat face, a stone balustrade and a large wrought-iron balcony above the front porch. Its windows were enormous, shining in the morning sun, set in precise rows across its face. She suspected that the rambling bit he had mentioned was at the back because she could just see a half-hidden wing to one side with much smaller windows set haphazard into its wall. And all around were green lawns and vast flower beds, so that she asked him, 'However many gardeners do you keep?'

He looked surprised. 'Two—oh, and a boy, I believe.'

'Don't you know?'

'I'm ashamed to say that there are several things I don't know about my own home—you see, of late I have been away a good deal; I leave things to Piet.'

Laura was beside him now, at the foot of the steps leading to the door. 'Piet?'

As if in answer to her question, the door opened and a portly man, no longer young, with white hair and very blue eyes, appeared on the top step. He beamed a welcome at Reilof, who shook him by the hand and exchanged some laughing greeting with him before saying, 'Well, Laura, you wanted to know who Piet was—this is he. He has been with my father and mother all their married life, and now he looks after me. I'm sure he will do the same for you.' He added reassuringly, 'He speaks English.'

Laura let out a little breath of relief and extended a hand. 'Oh, how very nice,' she exclaimed. 'How do you do, Piet.' She smiled at him and received a fatherly beam in return as he shook her hand.

'And if you are wondering why he isn't looking after my father instead of being here, I should tell you that his son performs that office.'

As he spoke Reilof had ushered her inside, leaving Piet to close the great door behind them, and she found herself in a square hall with doors on either side and a carved staircase at the back, flanked by arched doors presumably leading to the back of the house. It was a handsome and lofty apartment, its walls panelled in white-painted wood, picked out with gilt and lighted by delicate crystal wall sconces. A magnificent grandfather clock in a tulipwood case stood between two double doors on one side, and against the opposite wall was a side table in carved and gilded wood, flanked by two armchairs upholstered in needlework tapestry.

But she had little time to study these treasures, for Reilof took her arm and opened one of the double doors, urging her into a room, just as lofty and with two enormous windows draped in a rich terracotta velvet. The same colour was predominant in the Anatolian carpet and the comfortable chairs scattered about its vast floor; it was a pleasant contrast to the silvery wood with which the walls were panelled and the golden satinwood of the large rent table set between the windows. The same wood was used for the bow-fronted wall cabinets on either side of the marble fireplace, the silver and porcelain they displayed winking and glowing through their glass doors. There were a number of small tables, too, and another great wall cabinet of superb marquetry. A beautiful room, and Laura, pausing to take it all in on its threshold, was aware that all this magnificence was hers to live in now. It was a daunting thought, and she looked at Reilof with a touch of uncertainty.

'I hope you'll love it as much as I do,' he said gently, just as though he knew what she was thinking. 'This is the drawing room; we'll have our coffee and something to eat in the small sitting room, through here.'

He led her across to a narrow door by the fireplace which opened into a much smaller apartment, with Regency furniture and remarkably cosy, with its french windows opening on to a wide expanse of lawn, and chintz curtains blowing in the light breeze. The circular table in the centre of the room was laid with a snowy cloth and rose-patterned china, and two chairs had been drawn up to it most invitingly.

They were greeted here by Lucky, free of his plasters and a little stiff in his hind legs and his coat glossy and sleek, who got out of his basket and came to sniff delightedly at them, closely followed by an elderly sheepdog, stiff in the hind legs too, but from age. Laura made much of them both, and looked up to ask: 'Why Hovis?'

'He adores brown bread,' said Reilof. He put a hand on the old dog's head. 'The pair of them get on splendidly.'

The door opened then and a small, thin woman darted in, said something to Reilof and set a tray of coffee on the table. He answered her with a laugh and turned to Laura. 'This is Truus, Piet's wife—she looks after the house and does the cooking. I'm afraid she doesn't speak any English, but you will quickly learn some Dutch.'

Laura offered her hand once more and smiled and said how do you do, which she realised was rather silly, but what else was one to say?

Truus smiled and broke into speech again, and Reilof said: 'Truus says that she can see that you will be a good housewife and she welcomes a mistress to the house; she will be happy to work for you and to show you anything you may wish to see.'

Laura went a pretty pink. 'How kind! Please will you tell Truus that I shall value her friendship and help. It's generous of her to be so friendly—after all, I'm a complete stranger.'

'You are my wife.' Reilof spoke coolly and she wondered if she had annoyed him in some way. Perhaps he was reminding himself of the lovely bride he had expected to bring with him. Laura turned away to tickle Hovis's chin, for his woolly head was comforting under her hand and she needed comfort. There would be many more such moments before her, and the quicker she faced up to them without self-pity the better. Reilof, with Truus gone, asked her to pour their coffee and the face she turned to him was serene again; she had no intention of ever letting him see it otherwise.

They had their early lunch together, talking casually about nothing in particular, and when they had finished Reilof said shortly, 'You won't mind if I leave you? I have a good deal of work to attend to, I doubt if I shall be finished before the evening. I'll tell Truus to take you round the house. Piet will give you tea whenever you want it, and I daresay you want to unpack and have a rest. I have always had dinner at half-past seven, but if you would like to alter that time, please do as you think fit.'

Laura eyed him with surprise; he could have been addressing the new home help, but she forgave him. After all, he wasn't yet used to having a wife, if one could call her that. 'I don't expect I shall want to change anything,' she told him in a sensible voice, 'and if I did, I shouldn't dream of doing so until I consulted you and Truus.' She smiled a little. 'How wretched for you, having to plunge straight back into your work, though I daresay you don't mind at all. I'll see you this evening, then.'

He looked slightly taken aback as though he had expected her to complain at his going, although all he said was: 'I'll send Piet in as I go.'

Piet proved a mountain of helpfulness and common sense, and Laura found her afternoon gently organised for her. She should be taken at once to her room where she would find her clothes unpacked, and perhaps she would like an hour or so to herself, then perhaps Truus might come to her room at three o'clock and take her round the house. He would accompany them if Mevrouw had no objection, so that any questions she might wish to ask could be answered.

Laura smiled at the cheerful little man. 'That sounds perfect, Piet,' she told him. 'I'll go to my room now if Truus will take me there.'

She followed the housekeeper up the thickly-carpeted staircase and along a gallery which ran round three sides of the hall, and found her room to be at the front of the house, a large, light apartment with wide windows opening on to the wrought-iron balcony. A wide four poster bed was hung with the same pink and blue chintz as curtained the windows, and a delicate bow-fronted chest of satin-wood with painted panels stood against one wall. There was a sofa-table too between the windows, with a shieldback mirror upon it and elegant satin-wood chairs upholstered in pink striped silk, and on the bedside tables were exquisite china groups serving as lamps. Laura stood trying to take it all in. 'It's beautiful,' she said at length. 'I've never seen such a lovely room.' Her eyes roamed everywhere; it certainly lacked nothing, from its silk-striped pearly pink walls to the thick carpet under her feet, it was perfection itself.

'*De badkamer.*' Truus had opened a door cut into a wall to reveal a bathroom as modern and luxurious as any woman could wish for. Pink again, its shelves stocked with every soap and powder and lotion one could think of. Reilof would have bought these, Laura guessed, ready for Joyce's use. She wondered if Piet and Truus were surprised to find that his new wife was such a homely-looking girl with none of the sparkle attributed to a new bride, but when she thanked the housekeeper there was nothing in Truus's face to suggest it. It smiled back at her with genuine goodwill and a desire to please while the housekeeper got herself to the door with a few cheerful, unintelligible words. When she had gone, Laura had a leisurely bath, put on another dress and disdaining the desire for a nap, did her face and hair, this time allowing her mousy tresses to hang down her back, tied back with a chiffon scarf, and by the time she had done that there was a discreet knock on the door and Truus came in. Piet's voice from behind her said: 'If you are ready, *mevrouw*, we shall be most happy to show you the house.'

Perhaps they found it a little odd, mused Laura as she walked beside Truus along the gallery, that the doctor's new wife should be shown her new home by the housekeeper and not her husband. A vivid picture of Joyce arm-in-arm with Reilof, waltzing in and out of the rooms, discussing their furnishings, making him laugh, wheedling him to alter this and buy that, imprinted itself on her brain, but she frowned it away; Joyce mustn't be allowed to spoil any chance of happiness there might be for Reilof and herself, although perhaps contentment was the word she needed.

They inspected the rooms downstairs first; the drawing room, which she now went round at her leisure, the smaller sitting room behind it, the elegant dining room with its Hepplewhite chairs and table and massive side table. Twenty persons could sit down to dinner, Piet informed her with pride, and the dinner service used for such occasions was almost two hundred years old. Across the hall was the doctor's study; Laura didn't go in, but stood at the door, looking at the kneehole desk with its big, solid chair behind it, the shelves of books and the two leather armchairs drawn up to the hooded fireplace before going on to a small panelled room which Piet called the parlour, and much used, she fancied, for there was a small oval table in its centre with a magazine or two on it, a couple of books and a bowl of fresh flowers. The dogs' baskets were here too, as well as a charming little work-table with a button-backed balloon chair beside it.

Piet saw her looking at it and said at once, 'The doctor's mother used this room, *mevrouw*. She liked to have her tea here and sit quietly—he would come here each evening when she was alive...'

Which raised a problem. Would Reilof like her to use it too, or was it to be out of bounds? She would have to find out.

The kitchen premises last, said Piet firmly, leading the way upstairs again, past her own room, to open a neighbouring door with the words: 'The doctor's room, *mevrouw*.' A very masculine apartment it was, too, its mahogany furniture set off by a honey-coloured carpet and amber curtains and bedspread. Laura, feeling an intruder, glanced round, murmured appreciatively and turned her back on it to be shown the adjoining bathroom before passing on to the second side of the gallery. There were three rooms here, a good deal smaller than her own but large enough by her own standards, each furnished with great good taste, and along the third side there was a larger room again, with a narrow passage beside it running towards the back of the house. She had been right, the back wing rambled; the passage had corners, steps and unexpected windows and a great many rooms, some small, all exquisitely furnished, leading from it. She rather lost count of their number and the bathrooms which adjoined them, but there seemed a great number.

'The work!' she declared, round-eyed.

Truus understood her and smiled, but it was Piet who answered. 'These rooms are used only for guests,' he explained. 'At New Year and Christmas and when there is a family gathering. We have sufficient help in the house, *mevrouw*, and every modern aid to make the work light.'

Laura nodded. Reilof must have a great deal of money to live in a house of this size. Presumably, when he saw fit, he would tell her such details—after all, she was his wife, she had a right to know. She frowned; there were more and more problems cropping up to which she had given no thought at all.

The passage took a sharp turn and Truus opened the door which confronted them. '*Kinderkamer*,' she pronounced happily, and Piet said: 'Truus is very fond of children, *mevrouw*. This is the nursery —here is the day nursery, and here the sleeping rooms, three for the children, and one for the nurse-maid. The doctor's nanny lives here still—perhaps you knew that? She is old now but very sound in the head. She is at present in Scotland with her niece.'

He beamed at Laura and when she looked at Truus, Truus was smiling too. Presumably her arrival to them meant a nicely-filled nursery. The thought gave her a heartache; a number of little van Meerums romping around in the homely room would be exactly what the old house needed. She managed a smile, going a little pink in the face because she was, in a way, deceiving them. The pinkness made it worse; they exchanged happy, conspiratorial glances and shut the door with a satisfied click before escorting her up a narrow stair-case to the floor above—more bedrooms and a small sitting room, cosily furnished.

'Annie and Els, the two housemaids,' explained Piet, 'they have their rooms here, and there are also attics and store rooms and a bathroom. If you are not tired, *mevrouw*, we will go to the glass house.'

He meant the sun room, a vast one, running the width of the house at the back and entered from the small sitting room where they had had their lunch as well as a narrow door in the hall. It housed a variety of plants and flowers, and a white-painted table and chairs as well as comfortable loungers. It opened on to a wide lawn behind the house, surrounded by a herbaceous border, flowering shrubs and ornamental trees and there was a square pool in its centre with a little fountain playing. Laura gazed about her, taking in its beauty, conscious of a feeling of resentment that Reilof hadn't told her about it. Perhaps he had thought that she wouldn't be interested, perhaps he couldn't bear the thought of her enjoying something which Joyce would have revelled in. 'Luxury,' muttered Laura, and turned to listen to Piet explaining about the paths leading away from the lawn and into the shrubbery.

'There is a swimming pool on that side,' he waved an explanatory arm, 'and on this side there are the garages and outbuildings, and at the end of the garden there is a pretty summer house, very quiet. You like it, *mevrouw*?'

'Oh, I do,' declared Laura fervently, 'it's pure heaven.'

He gave her a kindly look. 'There is time enough for you to inspect the kitchens, *mevrouw*—you shall sit here and I will bring you the English afternoon tea. There is a pleasant seat near the fountain and a little table . . .'

She was pouring her first cup of Earl Grey from the gadrooned silver teapot when Piet came across the lawn once more, this time with a visitor. A thick-set young man of middle height, with lint-fair hair

116

and blue eyes in an open face. He smiled but didn't speak until Piet announced: 'Doctor Jan van Mijhof, the doctor's partner, *mevrouw*.' He added, 'I will bring another cup and saucer.'

Laura was on her feet, holding out a hand. 'Oh, how nice,' she exclaimed, 'I was feeling just a little lonely. Reilof told me about you, of course, but I didn't expect to meet you so soon.'

His smile broadened. 'For that I am guilty, Mevrouw van Meerum, I knew that Reilof would be back today. I am just returned from Amsterdam and I thought that I would call in on my way home. I expected that he would be here. Did some emergency make it necessary for him to work today?'

'I—I don't think so. He said that he had a great deal of work and wouldn't be back until this evening. I'm delighted that you called, though. Now I can have tea with someone . . .'

Piet had brought another cup and saucer and she bade her guest sit down while she poured his tea and offered him one of the little macaroons Truus had put on the tea tray. She had liked the young man at once; here, at least, was someone she would be able to talk to. He was about her own age, perhaps a little younger, and he had an open face which invited friendship.

'I've dozens of questions,' she said happily. 'You don't live here? Close by, I suppose? Do you share Reilof's consulting rooms, and do you have beds at the hospital too? And are you married . . .?'

Her companion laughed, although the look he

gave her was thoughtful; it seemed that Reilof hadn't told her much, which seemed strange, surely he would have told her these things long ago? All the same, he answered obligingly: 'I live in Baarn, and yes, I have a room at Reilof's consulting rooms, although he has by far the greater number of patients—he's well-known, you see, and much sought after. I'm lucky to be his partner, for I've only had a few years' post-graduate work, but when he offered me the partnership I jumped at it. I'm only a junior partner, of course, but I'm learning his ways and methods as quickly as I can.' He added reverently, 'He really is a splendid doctor and a fine man, *mevrouw*.' He refreshed himself with a macaroon and continued, 'I'm not married—at least, I should like to be ...' He looked suddenly shy and Laura said kindly:

'Will you tell me about it when you know me better?'

'I should like to—I don't want to bother Reilof—in fact, I haven't told anyone, only you.'

'Then I'll keep the secret,' she promised. 'Have some more tea and tell me how and where I can get someone to teach me Dutch.'

He gave her another thoughtful look. 'I expect Reilof knows of someone,' he suggested hesitantly, and when she just smiled, added boyishly: 'I say, Mevrouw van Meerum, I am very glad that Reilof has married. He is a marvellous man, you know, although it's silly for me to say that to you, isn't it?'

Laura said soberly: 'He's a very good man, and

by the way, since you and he are on christian name terms, could you call me Laura? I feel a hundred when you say Mevrouw van Meerum.'

They laughed together and were still laughing as Reilof came out of the house towards them. He was quite close before Laura looked up and saw him, and she called gaily, 'Oh, how nice, you're home for tea after all—I'll get another cup. Jan called to see you and stayed to keep me company.'

Reilof gave her a bland look which concealed she knew not what. 'So I see—don't bother about another cup, I had coffee at the hospital.' He took a handful of Truus's macaroons and sat down to eat them. 'How are you, Jan?' His voice was friendly, but the bland look was still there; he was annoyed about something and she didn't know what. Of course, she could be imagining that; she would have to be a little less sensitive, and indeed, there was nothing it his manner to bear out her suspicion.

He stayed talking to Jan about their holiday for ten minutes or so and then suggested that they went to his study so that they might discuss some patient's treatment. His, 'I'll be back shortly, my dear,' was exactly the remark any wife might expect from a husband. She watched their retreating backs, relaxing in the sunshine. Jan was nice. His 'goodbye, Laura,' had been friendly and just a shade differential, which amused her very much; of course she was his partner's wife ... She mused gently about nothing in particular, and presently closed her eyes and slept.

119

She was surprised to find that she had been asleep for almost an hour. The tea tray had gone and the two dogs, who had been sitting with her, were nowhere to be seen. Perhaps Reilof had come back, decided not to disturb her, and gone back to the house. But when she went indoors there was no sign of him; she went in search of Piet finally, and he told her in some surprise that the doctor was in his study and that Doctor van Mijhof had been gone for half an hour or more. His look registered polite surprise that she hadn't been to see for herself, and she said hastily: 'I'll not disturb him, he's bound to be busy,' very conscious that a newly-married man, however busy he might be, might be expected to welcome a visit from his bride, and went to her room. There was more than an hour to dinner, so she occupied it in changing her dress for the honey-coloured jersey and sweeping her hair up into its tidy bun once more.

There was no one in the drawing room when she went down, nor in the little sitting room behind it, and she sat down by the open window and leafed through a Dutch newspaper to no purpose at all and feeling lonely. Reilof's quiet, 'Hullo, so there you are,' from the open door took her by surprise, so that she dropped the paper all over the floor and uttered a feeble, 'I wasn't sure where to go ...'

He raised his eyebrows. 'Anywhere you wish, Laura. I usually work in my study for an hour before dinner and again afterwards. I'm afraid I keep late hours, but that shouldn't bother you.' He added surprisingly, 'You've put your hair up.'

She decided to ignore that. 'It won't bother me in the least,' she assured him cheerfully as she accepted a glass of sherry. 'At what time do you have breakfast?'

'Half-past seven. If that is too early for you, one of the maids will bring it to your room, or you can come down later.'

She felt like an unwelcome guest being treated with the minimum of good manners. 'I shouldn't dream of putting anyone to the trouble,' she told him, a thought snappish. 'Breakfast at half-past seven suits me very well. You won't need to talk to me, you know.'

He looked surprised and then laughed. 'I'm sorry, I didn't mean to be so ill-humoured. I suppose I'm not used to being married again.'

'I know exactly what you mean,' she told him kindly. 'I feel a bit the same myself. But don't imagine that I shall interfere with your life or your habits—I told you that I wouldn't and I won't, only you must tell me when I get in the way or do something to vex you, otherwise I shan't know.'

He put down his glass and came to stand before her. 'Laura, you're a nice girl and an understanding one. Give me a little time, will you? And I promise you that I'll tell you when you vex me, and you must do the same. Shall we go in to dinner?'

He pulled her to her feet and tucked an arm into hers so that her heart bounced against her ribs. 'Tell me, what did you think of the house?'

Getting ready for bed later that evening, she decided that the evening had been a success; they had enjoyed their meal together and Reilof had told her something of his work at the hospital and a little, but not much, about his private practice. And later he had telephoned his father and arranged for them to drive over to see him the following evening, so that she was able to see him go to his study and wish him a placid goodnight without too much disappointment. After all, he had warned her that he worked each evening, and she had their visit to his father to look forward to. 'Count your blessings, my girl,' she admonished her reflection, and jumped into her enormous bed, to sleep at once and dream of Reilof.

CHAPTER SEVEN

REILOF was already at the breakfast table when Laura got down the following morning, deep in his letters and with a newspaper spread out before him as well. Evidently not a chatty meal—she wished him a quiet good morning and sat down opposite him, accepting the English newspapers laid neatly beside her plate as a strong hint to maintain silence. She poured herself some coffee; Reilof, who got to his feet as she went in, had returned to his mail once more, sparing a few seconds to hope that she had slept well and inviting her to help herself to anything she wanted and ring for anything she wished. She rather fancied that he didn't hear her polite 'Thank you,' and he didn't speak again until he had finished his letters, when he swallowed his coffee and rose to his feet once more.

'I expect to be home about six,' he told her, and halfway to the door remembered to wish her a pleasant day.

'Doing what?' asked Laura silently to his disappearing back, and then remembered that he had asked her to have patience. As it turned out there was plenty to occupy her time; the kitchens to inspect—a roomy complex with a separate scullery and laundry, and what she supposed was the Dutch equivalent of a butler's pantry. She met the two maids, too, Annie and Els, strapping young girls who smiled widely as they greeted her and then the gardener, an old man with a weatherbeaten face and a fringe of white hair, and when she had had her coffee in the sun room she was borne away to inspect linen cupboards, kitchen equipment and the house-keeping books. The latter made almost no sense at all, but she felt it was incumbent on her to make a start. The amount of money spent on food rather staggered her, but presumably Reilof could afford it, although when she changed the guldens into pounds the total made her open her eyes.

And after her solitary lunch she went to the swimming pool and spent a lazy hour. She swam well and the pool was a good size and the water warm, then she dressed and had tea in the garden, then went up to her room to change her dress, ready for Reilof's return.

They were to dine with his father, he had told her, and she put on one of her new dresses, a silk print in shades of green, sleeveless and nicely cut, adding the Charles Jourdan sandals which she hadn't really been able to afford because she wanted to make a good impression. But they made no impression on Reilof when he came home; he put his head round the sitting room door, said, 'Hullo—shan't keep you long,' and went straight upstairs to reappear presently in a pale grey checked suit and a rather splendid tie. She doubted very much if he had any idea at all of what she was wearing, and he barely glanced at her as he suggested briskly that they should leave immediately.

Laura got to her feet at once, wished the dogs goodbye and accompanied Reilof out to the car—the Aston Martin this time—and he didn't speak at all until they were through Hilversum and almost at Loenen. 'You don't have much to say for yourself,' he observed a little impatiently.

'I have plenty to say for myself,' declared Laura with asperity, 'but only when people want to listen to me. If you wish me to greet you,' she went on with some heat, 'with a flow of small talk of an evening, you have only to say so. I didn't get that impression when you came home just now.'

'My dear good girl, you don't have to fly at me like a wildcat! You are free to say what you want and when you want to say it, you know.'

'That isn't what you said, you told me that you didn't want your present way of living changed.' She stared out of the window at the pretty country they were passing through and added without looking at him, 'I haven't taken umbrage, only made myself clear.'

His voice was silky. 'Very clear, Laura. You sound exactly like a wife.'

She nipped back the answer to that just in time and held her tongue with an effort, until in a silence grown too long she observed sweetly:

'How pretty it is here.'

'Delightful.'

They were on a narrow road running alongside a

lake of some size. There were boats of all shapes and sizes moored at its edge, and on the other side of the road were handsome villas, each standing in its own spacious grounds, screened from the road by shrubs and trees and well-clipped hedges.

It was through the gate of one of these houses that Reilof drove the car, to stop before the already open door of a fair-sized house with a thatched roof with a patio, screened by climbing roses, at one side.

'Oh, very pretty,' exclaimed Laura, refusing to be damped by Reilof's silence, and jumped out before he could get round to open her door, but he caught her by the arm as they went up the path so that at a distance at least they must have looked like a devoted pair. And so it must have seemed to the man waiting for them at the door—Piet's son, looking just like a younger version of his father—for he smiled in a pleased way as Reilof introduced him to her and said in rather quaint English: 'It is a great delight that you enter the van Meerum family, *mevrouw*,' before leading them across the dim, cool hall to a room at the back of the house which overlooked a formal garden, its doors wide to the summer evening.

Its only occupant got to his feet as they went in and came to meet them; an elderly man with iron-grey hair and dark eyes, as tall as his son and as broad too, but unlike his son he was smiling. He said: 'Reilof ... and your Laura,' and then turned to put his hands on her shoulders and kiss her cheek. 'My dear girl, I am so happy to welcome you into the family.' He held her away a little and studied her face while she stayed quiet under his look. 'I have always wanted another daughter,' he told her kindly, 'and now I have a charming one. I am glad that Reilof brought you here to meet me before he shows you off to the rest of the family.'

He took her arm and led her to an enormous sofa. 'Come and sit down and tell me about yourself. Reilof, will you get us all a drink? Dinner will be in about half an hour.'

The evening was a huge success; Laura, completely at ease with the elder of her two companions, wondered why it was that Reilof didn't allow himself to show the charm which his father demonstrated so easily. That he had charm she was well aware, and on one or two occasions during the evening he did relax, so that they were all talking and laughing like old friends with no hint of restraint, but the barrier he had put between them was there again once they were on their way home again. He refused to be drawn into more than polite, brief comments on their evening, despite her efforts, so that by the time they had arrived home once more she could find nothing more to do than wish him goodnight.

They were to go again to his father's house later in the week, and the rest of the family would be there too—a celebration dinner, old Doctor van Meerum had told Laura. She was to wear her prettiest dress and perhaps they would clear the drawing room of its furniture and dance afterwards.

It had all sounded fun, but thinking about it the next morning she wasn't so sure; supposing none of them liked her?

She went down to her breakfast feeling subdued, and was made more so by Reilof's announcement that he would be going to Maastricht for a seminar and would be away for two days. 'I believe that I did mention that I go away frequently for a day or two at a time,' he observed, 'but I'm sure that you'll find plenty to do—get Piet to drive you if you want to do any shopping in den Haag or Amsterdam. You have enough money?'

'Yes, thank you, Reilof.' She tried to make her voice cheerful. Of course she had plenty of money, he had been more than generous with her allowance; she had never had so much money to spend on herself in her life before—only she would have forgone the lot in exchange for just one gift from him, something he had bought himself. Not even a wedding present, she told herself forlornly, and remembered the gold cufflinks she had bought for him and had hidden away in a drawer when she realised that he had no thought of giving her anything.

'I don't think I shall need to bother Piet; there's heaps for me to see in Hilversum and Baarn, and the bus service is awfully good.'

He looked surprised. 'Oh, is it? I don't have occasion to use it.' He got up and came round the table to her chair and surprisingly bent to kiss her cheek. 'Piet will look after you,' he told her. '*Tot ziens*.'

He left her sitting there while the two dogs bustled along at his heels to see him off. Given the slightest encouragement Laura would have seen him off too, but she wasn't given any.

She filled the two days somehow, writing letters, exploring Baarn and Hilversum, shopping a little, spending long hours in the garden with her head bent over the embroidery she had bought to keep her occupied. There were the dogs to take for walks too, and Truus to consult about meals, but all the same she thought about Reilof almost all the time, wondering what he was doing and who he was with. It was strange to love a man so much and know so little about him.

He came back very late on the evening of the second day; she had been in bed for an hour or more and it had struck midnight before she heard the car turn into the drive and stop. Laura skipped out of bed at once and peeped from her window to see Reilof enter the house, and presently she heard him come upstairs and go to his room. She shivered a little by the open window and got back into bed; it would have been nice to have gone downstairs and made him a drink or sandwiches, but he might not have liked that. All the same, it was lovely to have him home again—she would ask him about Dutch lessons in the morning. She had half expected him to mention them, but perhaps he had been too busy ... She drifted off into a daydream in which she learned to speak Dutch with a faultless accent and surprised and delighted him with her brilliance, and presently she went to sleep.

She brought the matter up at breakfast and was agreeably surprised when he said instantly: 'Yes, of course you shall have lessons—I know just the man to teach you, too. I'll telephone him this morning and arrange it. At what time of the day would you like him to come?'

Laura considered: she spent an agreeably pleasant hour in the kitchen with Truus after breakfast and then another hour walking the dogs. 'Eleven o'clock?' she wondered out loud. 'I should like to learn Dutch as quickly as possible. I did ask Jan about lessons, but he said you would be bound to arrange something ...'

'You asked Jan ... ?' There was no mistaking the annoyance in his voice, although he looked placid enough.

'Well, yes—you see, I don't see you very often, really, do I? And you're busy.'

He let that pass and gathered up his letters. 'I'll arrange for eleven o'clock each day except Saturday and Sunday. Mijnheer de Wal can come here.'

'Does he have far to come? If he lives in Baarn or Hilversum I could easily catch a bus ...'

Reilof was ready to go. 'I prefer him to come to the house,' he said briefly. 'I shall be home just before tea.'

So she began lessons with Mijnheer de Wal, a nice old gentleman with a luxurious moustache and beard, a benign expression and a firm determination to teach her to speak correct Dutch if it was the last thing he should do. After the first lesson she rather enjoyed herself, took his stern corrections meekly and made peculiar mistakes which she longed to laugh about with Reilof. But he, beyond asking her if she had started her lessons, made no further inquiries as to her progress, so that at the end of the week, when they were bidden to his father's house, she was able to surprise him by uttering a handful of painstakingly correct phrases, learned especially for the occasion.

And it had been an occasion, a red-letter day to be looked back on with pleasure. Reilof had asked her to wear her wedding dress, and, rather mystified, she had done so, and when she had gone downstairs he had been waiting for her in the drawing room, very elegant in his dinner jacket. He had stared at her rather as though he had never seen her before, before opening a leather case on the table beside him.

'I asked you to wear that dress because it would provide a suitable background for these,' he said. 'Stand still a moment.'

He had hung a necklace round her neck, a magnificent affair of rubies set around with diamonds, and then turned her round to see her reflection in the big Chippendale mirror on one wall. She was gasping with surprise when he lifted her hand and clasped a matching bracelet round her wrist.

She looked at that too, her eyes round with excitement and delight.

'They're gorgeous!' she managed. 'I suppose ...'

'These too, but you'll have to put them on for yourself.'

The earrings were pear-shaped drops of rubies and diamonds in a heavy gold setting, and she poked the hooks into her ears and swung her head from side to side, admiring them. Her eyes met his in the mirror and she smiled widely and then turned towards him. 'Thank you, Reilof—I've never had...'

His matter-of-fact, 'The eldest son's wife inherits them. I can hardly take the credit for giving them to you,' damped her delight as effectively as a bucket of water would have done. She said bleakly, 'Oh, I see—and of course I have to wear them this evening...'

'Just so. Are we ready?'

But despite that unhappy little episode, the evening had been a success. Her father-in-law liked her and Margriet, Reilof's sister, had been charming and kind and friendly too. She was a pretty girl in her thirties, with his dark eyes, and her husband, a tall, bony man, good-looking in a rangy way, treated her with a casual warmth which she had found very reassuring. As for Laurent, the youngest of the family, he made no bones about liking her on sight; they had got on famously and were instant friends, so that the evening which she had been dreading had proved to be the greatest fun.

There had been uncles and aunts too, and half a dozen cousins, all making much of her, and after the family dinner party, friends had come in for drinks and to offer congratulations. Laura stood beside Reilof, shaking dozens of friendly hands, very conscious of him and the hand he had tucked under her arm from time to time. She had done her best; presumably his family, though perhaps not his father, thought that Reilof had married her for love and not just on an impulse, and she had behaved, she hoped, just as she ought, unaware that each time she had looked at him her love showed so clearly that all the members of the van Meerum family had gone home delighted that Reilof had fallen in love with a girl who so obviously adored him.

And Reilof—his behaviour couldn't be faulted. He had said and done exactly the right things, smiling pleasantly as they had talked with first one and then the other of the family, and he had smiled at her too, his eyes dark and expressionless, so that she had felt cold inside. But when they were home again he observed pleasantly enough that everyone had liked her and she had been a great success with the family. She had thanked him quietly, wishing that he could like her and more than that, and then went upstairs in her magnificent jewels, sparkling in the light from the chandelier, and cried herself to sleep.

But there was no point in wishing for the moon; she was Reilof's wife and sooner or later she was determined to win his regard and even his love. She was beginning to fit nicely into his life now; she got on well with Truus, and Piet was her devoted slave; she had taken over a number of small chores about the house, gone shopping, and armed with the necessary basic Dutch Mijnheer de Wal dinned into her, coped with the telephone, callers, and the wives of Reilof's colleagues, who came to see what see was like. Because she was friendly and unassuming and a little shy they liked her, a fact which Reilof remarked upon one evening at dinner.

'Quite a success,' he told her blandly. 'You have slipped into your new role very easily, Laura.'

She wasn't sure if he was being deliberately nasty. 'Your family have been more than kind to me. I have a lot to thank them for—your friends too. And Mijnheer de Wal is a wonderful teacher, and Jan gives me lots of tips ...'

'Jan?' Reilof was on his way to his study.

She had got up from the table with him. 'Well, yes—I see him from time to time, you know.'

His eyebrows lifted. 'Indeed? You like him?'

'Oh, very much ...' She noticed then that his dark eyes were studying her closely. She added lamely, 'He makes me laugh.'

He crossed the hall without a word and went into his study, closing the door very quietly behind him.

It was a couple of days later that he came home in the afternoon. Laura had been sitting in the garden, lounging on the grass with the two dogs and learning Dutch verbs, and was quite unprepared for his unexpected appearance, strolling across the grass with his hands in his pockets. She got to her feet at once, exclaiming happily, 'How lovely, you're early!'

He bent to fondle the dogs. 'Yes—if you're not

busy doing anything special, I should like to show you something.'

She cast her books on one side. 'Grammar,' she told him, 'and I'm sick of it—it's a frightful language. Of course I'll come.'

They went round the side of the house where the garages were; a converted coach-house with a broad sweep before it. All three garage doors were open. The Rolls and the Aston Martin were snugly stowed away, and outside the third was a small Fiat, new and shining and bright blue. 'Yours,' said Reilof.

'Mine?' Laura choked a little with excitement. 'Reilof, what an absolutely super present! Thank you ...'

He glanced at her briefly. 'Hardly a present, more a necessity, I should have said.'

All her lovely excitement faded, and if it had been physically possible she would have picked up the little car and flung it at him. Instead she contented herself with an airy, 'How kind—I shall enjoy going around on my own.' She almost added, 'As usual,' but thought better of it. She was wandering round the bonnet as she spoke and didn't see the look of faint surprise on his face as he suggested:

'Why not try her out now?'

'Now? But the traffic's on the wrong side of the road ... I shall have to get used to it.'

'So you will,' he agreed mildly, although there was a glimmer of laughter in his eyes. 'Why not run her down to the gate and get the feel of her?'

He was holding the door open for her to get in

and it seemed a good idea. With him beside her, she started the engine and rather gingerly drove to the gate, and when she reached it he said in a no-nonsense voice: 'We might as well go to Hilversum —take your time and get across to the other lane.'

She was speechless; a little scared and cross at the trick he had played on her, but she did as she was told because pride wouldn't let her do anything else. His, 'Good girl, nicely done,' mollified her a little, but as he followed it with: 'Don't strangle the wheel, let it run through your hands, otherwise when you get to a corner you won't have a hand left,' a criticism which made her say tartly, 'I can drive, you know,' and then because it was rather fun driving her very own car with Reilof beside her, she laughed. 'It's super!'

'That's better—you're doing very well. We'll call on Father, he thinks you're a girl in a million and here's your chance to prove it.'

She changed gear with a clash. What was the use of her father-in-law prizing her so highly when his son did not? She put her foot down and the car shot forward too fast, and Reilof said on an unperturbed chuckle, 'He'd like to see you in one piece, though.'

She drove the rest of the way with exaggerated care and no further comments from Reilof, and the old gentleman's delighted welcome should have soothed her ruffled feelings, but Reilof, charming as ever, remained aloof from the small jokes and con-gratulations, just as though it didn't matter to him whether she could drive or not. When they got home his, 'You did quite well, Laura, but don't go out on your own yet,' did nothing to make her feel better.

'You're almost never home,' she pointed out waspishly, 'and when you are you're too busy to bother . . .'

He stared at her for a long moment. 'Ah—I neglect you, Laura?' he asked silkily.

'I didn't say that. I'm stating a fact, that's all—you told me you'd have very little time for me,' she reminded him.

They were standing outside the front door and she felt at a disadvantage because she had to look up at him. She said quickly, 'Well, it doesn't matter, you know, I'm not throwing it in your teeth or anything like that.'

His smile enchanted her, for it was unexpected and just for a moment he looked different, almost as though he liked her very much. She said breathlessly to fill the silence between them, 'I'm sorry if I was beastly.'

His arm caught her round the waist and clamped her tight. 'Never that,' he said softly, 'long-suffering, patient, understanding, but never beastly.' He kissed her suddenly and hard and then released her, opened the door, ushered her inside, then said: 'I've a patient to see—I'll see you at dinner.'

But at dinner there was a message to say that he had been called to the hospital and she wasn't to wait. Laura went to bed early and lay awake for a long time thinking about his kiss; it hadn't been like the routine peck he occasionally gave her. Perhaps there was the very beginnings of a chance . . .

It was going to be a remote one, she realised the next morning, for Reilof wished her a good day with his usual cool pleasantness and told her at once that he would be away lecturing in Brussels, for three days this time. The salute he bestowed on her cheek as he went was as impersonal and brief as the conventional salute one would give an aunt whom one disliked, so that when he said curtly, 'Don't go out in the Fiat alone, Laura,' her mood was ripe to ask him huffily why not.

'Because I ask you not to,' he said, making it worse. He had closed the door behind him before she had an answer ready.

She went about her quiet life as usual after he had gone while she allowed the idea that he had no right to order her about to fester in the back of her mind. She was, after all, a fairly good driver and no headstrong teenager. By the third day she had convinced herself that he had told her not to drive the Fiat because he was bossy and arrogant, and by the time lunch was finished she was so convinced of this that she went to the garage, took the car out and drove it out of the gate and on to the main road. She was a little vague as to where she would go; she was in the lane to Hilversum, so she might as well go shopping. She still had almost all of the allowance Reilof had given her and some new clothes might make her feel better, she told herself, and put her foot down hard on the accelerator.

Plans for this buoyed her up through the intricacies of getting herself to the heart of the town, and she was almost there when her eye caught a sign to Amsterdam—and why not? she asked herself, turning the Fiat into the side street it indicated. It was quieter here and led to a still quieter street, with narrow houses and a canal running through its centre; she guessed that it would bring her sooner or later to the main Amsterdam road and slackened her pace, ignoring the faint feeling of guilt she hadn't quite got rid of, pleased with herself and almost happy.

Reilof, just back unexpectedly a day early from his lectures and standing idly at the window of his consulting room, was watching the street below while he waited for the first patient of the afternoon, and seeing the Fiat going past he felt neither of these sensations, however. He stared at the little blue car, with Laura's profile and mousy head of hair just visible, and then exploded into forceful Dutch as he strode from the room. His secretary was alone in the reception room and gaped in surprise when he told her harshly that he was called away urgently.

'The patients?' she wanted to know.

'Make new appointments—telephone, do anything you think fit—I leave them in your capable hands, Willa. I'll telephone you later. Go home as usual if I'm not back.'

Willa, middle-aged, cosy and highly efficient, persisted doggedly, 'But where are you going, doctor?'

He was halfway through the door. 'I haven't the faintest idea.'

Laura was on the motorway, Hilversum behind

her, heading for Amsterdam, and by now she rather regretted her impulse. The traffic was heavy and very fast; she crept to the slow lane and stayed in it while huge juggernauts, speed fiends and long-distance transports sped past her. But she kept a steady pace, not allowing them to upset her, so that when there was a splintering crash a hundred yards ahead of her and a car somersaulted across the fast lane and cannoned across it to the shoulder of the motorway, she had ample time to drive on to the shoulder too, and stop. Miraculously, there didn't seem to be any other car involved, indeed the traffic was streaming ahead as though nothing had happened, so that she was the only person to reach the upside-down car. There was one occupant, suspended upside down too from his seat by his safety belt, and fully conscious.

She couldn't understand a word he said, of course. She made haste to say in her careful, slow Dutch, 'I'm English—speak slowly, I don't understand Dutch very well.' It was a great relief when he said in tolerable English: 'My legs are held . . .'

They were indeed, and it would take more than her strength to help him. She looked over her shoulder in some desperation and saw that several cars had stopped now and men were running towards the wreck. Nice, strong men, she saw with relief; they would need all their strength to roll the car back on to its wheels without hurting the man trapped inside. 'For heaven's sake, take care,' she begged them, heedless of the fact that they might not understand what she was saying, and peered in once at the unfortunate driver. 'Hold on to the seat,' she warned him. 'They'll be as careful as they can, but you're bound to bounce a bit.'

He bounced a lot before they were finished, and was unconscious as the men hauled him carefully out on to the grass verge. Laura looked at his pale, sweaty face and felt a feeble pulse before asking for a penknife from her willing helpers and slitting a trouser leg, urging someone to do the same with the second one. She did it slowly and with great patience, presently exposing a badly crushed limb, so engrossed in her task that she neither saw nor heard the Rolls pull up silently within yards of her.

'My God, I'll talk to you later,' said Reilof with soft fury in her ear, adding in an impersonal, professional voice: 'Hold that foot steady and I'll do what I can,' and after one look at his white, set face, she did as she was told without a word. He had his bag with him and began to work on the leg, giving brief orders to the other men as he did so, and ignoring Laura except to give her even briefer instructions from time to time. The ambulance and police had arrived by the time both legs had been dealt with and Laura, no longer needed, stood on one side watching them load the victim into the ambulance and drive away while the police went from one to the other of the men, taking statements. They knew Reilof, something she was thankful for when it came to her turn, for she told her part in the episode to him and he repeated it in his own language. When she had finished he took her arm and said, 'Will you get into the car? I'll be with you in a moment, I must get someone to drive the Fiat back.'

'I can ...' she began, caught his dark gaze and got meekly into the Rolls. His expression had been inscrutable, but that cold stare had warned her that he was in a very nasty temper. She braced herself for a forceful outburst—quite unnecessarily, for he drove all the way home without saying a word. Only as they went into the house he said at his silkiest: 'A moment of your time, Laura.'

She went past him into the study and took the bull by the horns.

'You came back a day early ...'

He ignored this obvious remark. 'I asked you not to drive the Fiat on your own, Laura.' He drew a chair forward. 'Will you not sit down?'

'No,' said Laura, 'I'd rather stand, and you didn't ask me, you know, you ordered me in the most arrogant way.'

'My apologies. Is that why you did it?'

She said honestly, 'Yes, I think it was. You see, I'm not a bad driver and I'm not a silly young girl.'

'No, just a silly one,' he observed icily. 'When I saw you drive past my consulting rooms just now, I ...' He paused. 'Well, never mind that now—perhaps you can imagine my feelings when I saw the Fiat on the shoulder and you nowhere in sight.'

Laura was still recovering from being called a silly girl so scathingly. She said furiously, 'No, I

142

can't imagine your feelings—you haven't any for me, anyway. And now if you've quite finished lecturing me, I'll go to my room. I have a headache.'

He took a step towards her. 'Laura, you weren't hurt?'

She turned her back and made for the door, longing to have a nice long cry in peace and quiet. 'No, but it would have served me right if I had been, wouldn't it?' She slammed the door after her and raced upstairs and banged her bedroom door too, and when Els came to see if she would like a tray of tea she refused it and moreover told her to let the doctor know that she wouldn't be coming down to dinner—a high-handed decision she regretted later when her normally healthy appetite made itself felt. There was a tin of biscuits beside her bed, so she ate the lot and washed them down with water from the bathroom while she thought with longing of the carefully-chosen menu she and Truus had decided upon that morning. She took a long time over her bath, washed her hair and experimented with her make-up, and it was still only a little after nine o'clock. Presently she got into bed, to lie awake listening for Reilof to go to his room. He still hadn't come when it struck midnight, and worn out with hunger and the reaction from the afternoon's adventure, she fell asleep.

Dressing the next morning, she had the vague idea of apologising over breakfast; she didn't see why she should, but on the other hand, someone would have to offer the olive branch. But when she sat down opposite him to face his cold politeness and hard eyes, she quailed. They ate in silence and it was a relief when Reilof got to his feet with the remark that he would be in for lunch, and strode from the room. Laura did her small morning chores, gave only half her attention to Mijnheer de Wal and the subtleties of the past tense, and went into the garden with the dogs.

It was here that Jan found her; he had called to leave a patient's case notes for Reilof to advise on, and stayed to pass the time of day with her. It was almost lunchtime by now, but Piet brought more coffee and they sat together by the swimming pool, talking easily about nothing much until Jan said, 'I haven't liked to ask you before, Mevrouw van Meerum, but I think perhaps you could help me ...'

Laura turned to look at him. His face was earnest and worried and she said warmly, 'Of course I will, but only if you call me Laura. What's the matter?'

'Well, I wish very much to marry and I would like to tell Reilof about it. You see, when he took me as his partner, he allowed me to live in a small flat he has in Baarn—just right for me, for the surgery is close by—and he told me that if I should want to marry, he would let me have a house which he owns, also in Baarn. Now that is splendid, is it not? But Ella, the girl I wish to marry, is refusing to do this. She says that I must buy a house of my own, not live in one which Reilof has given me. She will not marry me unless I have a home of my own, for she says that he will expect me to work harder and do

144

more for him, and that he will take advantage of me. I know that this is nonsense; we are great friends although Reilof is so much older than I, but I cannot make her see ... it would be between friends, you understand. I would do the same for him if I were in his place. I wonder if you would talk to her, make her see that he would never do a mean thing to anyone. And perhaps you could suggest to Reilof that I might buy the house from him—it would take me years, of course, and he will not like it, for he has a great deal of money and knows that I have only my income. You think that I should see him about this, but he is absorbed in his work, and besides, now he has you to absorb his thoughts and days.'

Laura smiled wryly. 'So he has. Of course I'll help. Where does your Ella live?'

'In Utrecht. I have to go there tomorrow and I wondered if you would come with me—and talk to her?'

'A splendid idea. In the morning? I'll go to work on her and then perhaps you could talk to Reilof. I know just how your Ella feels, but if you could persuade him to let you buy the house—and you'll have years in which to do that, won't you?—that should solve the problem. But first we have to make Ella see. Now, what time ...?'

They had their heads together as Reilof came across the garden towards them, so engrossed in times and meeting places that they didn't know he was there until Hovis and Lucky came out of the shrubbery to rush barking towards him. They turned slightly guilty faces towards him in consequence, the effect made worse by Jan jumping up, declaring that he had to be off at once and that he had left his patient's notes in Reilof's study and would see his partner later on in the day.

Reilof saw him off the premises with his usual friendliness, and rather to Laura's surprise didn't mention him at all during lunch. Instead he kept up a steady flow of nothings, as though he was determined to be pleasant at all costs however difficult it might be, and presently left Laura to go back to his consulting rooms, leaving her puzzled; he had been annoyed when he had found her and Jan in the garden and even though he had been at his pleasantest during lunch, he had looked at her searchingly once or twice and the annoyance was still there, although well concealed.

It was a hot and airless morning when Laura got up the next day, and over breakfast Reilof told her that he would certainly be late home, information which couldn't have pleased her better, for she had agreed to meet Jan at ten o'clock in Baarn. She caught the local bus without hindrance, met him at the arranged spot and was soon being driven to Utrecht, sitting beside him in his Citroën as she listened with a sympathetic ear to the ups and downs of his courtship of Ella.

That young lady proved to be quite charming; small and fair and blue-eyed and, Laura suspected, with an iron will of her own which Jan quite rightly didn't intend to give in to. Now she could see why he had asked her help; he wanted to marry his Ella on his own terms and not on hers. He had left them together over coffee in one of the big cafés with the promise that he would return and take them out to lunch at half-past twelve, and the coffee pot empty, Laura suggested that they might go somewhere quiet where they could talk. It hadn't occurred to her that Ella might not speak English, but now she thanked heaven that her knowledge of the language was so good, for it would make it much easier to explain about the house and Jan's wishes.

It made her feel rather old, giving advice about husbands to this pretty creature, especially as she knew so little about them herself, but she put the case clearly and in such a matter-of-fact way that before long Ella was at least prepared to rearrange her ideas. Over lunch, Laura was happy to see that Jan, if he was tactful and in no hurry, would get his own way. He seemed to think so too, for he was in great good spirits on their way back, and when he dropped her off outside her own front door, he got out of the car with her, and although he refused an invitation to come inside, he gave her a hug and kiss and told her she was a fairy godmother to them both.

'Good,' laughed Laura. 'Now all you have to do is to make quite sure of Ella and then go and see Reilof.'

He nodded. 'You won't say anything to him yet?'

'No, I won't—Ella still needs a little coaxing; you want her on your side before you do anything more.'

He was about to kiss her again when the house door opened and Reilof strolled out and Laura, utterly taken aback, said with an aplomb which amazed her, 'Oh, hullo—Jan has just brought me back from Utrecht. He was going there and I wanted to do some shopping.'

He smiled without saying anything, a very nasty smile, and she added hastily as he allowed his eyes to roam over the car, 'But I didn't buy anything.' She turned to Jan. 'Thanks for the lift—I expect I'll see you some time.'

'I'll see you at the hospital this evening,' cut in Reilof, at his pleasantest, 'that meeting at nine o'clock,' and Jan said hastily, 'Oh, yes—I hadn't forgotten. *Tot ziens.*' He got into his car and drove off, waving as he went.

Laura went indoors with Reilof and as he shut the door, he asked: 'You had a pleasant day?'

'Very nice, thank you.'

'You didn't expect me back until the evening?'

'No—you said you would be late.'

'I hope I haven't disturbed any plans you may have made with Jan?'

'Plans? Me? With Jan?' She choked on surprise. 'What plans could I possibly have with him?'

'Certainly not shopping in Utrecht,' he commented silkily. 'That was a lie, wasn't it, Laura?' He was standing in the centre of the hall, watching her.

'Yes,' she said steadily, 'it was, and I can't explain it. Why are you so angry and suspicious, Reilof?'

He smiled then. 'You would be surprised if I

told you why; I'm surprised myself.' He came nearer. 'Laura, is it too late for us to try and regain the friendship we first had? It has been my fault; I've treated you badly, anyone other than you would have washed their hands of me long ago, instead of which you've run my home to perfection, charmed my family and friends, made devoted slaves of my servants and struggled to learn my language.' He paused. 'Do you regret marrying me?'

She longed to tell him just how little she regretted it, but she kept her voice level and friendly. 'No, I don't regret that, Reilof, and I can't see why we shouldn't be friends. You—your life has been upset and I realise that it made you difficult sometimes.' She smiled at him. 'Let's try again. You know, just now, when you came out of the house I thought you were blazing with rage . . .'

His dark eyes glinted. 'Now I wonder why you should have thought that? Have you had tea, or shall we have it in the garden?'

Sometimes the gods were kind, thought Laura. She must seize her chances of happiness whenever she could—this was one of them.

'I'm famished,' she told him happily. 'We'll go by the pool, shall we? Truus made one of her gorgeous cakes this morning and I could eat it all!'

CHAPTER EIGHT

A WEEK went by, and at its end Laura, reflecting upon it, nodded her head with satisfaction; at least she and Reilof hadn't fallen out once, or worse than that, ignored each other. He had found time to sit beside her while she drove the Fiat to the Hague to visit his sister, and taken time off to arrange for her to take a driving test; he had even taken her to his consulting rooms to meet the faithful Willa, shown her his surgery and the hospital where he had beds and explained about his lecture tours. It was as though he intended to admit her to part of his life at least, although he wore an air of thoughtful reserve which had prevented her from being anything but pleasantly friendly. She had contented herself in responding readily but without eagerness to any suggestions he had made for their mutual entertainment, and had done a little quiet shopping for a new dress or two, had her mousy hair becomingly dressed and indulged in a whole new stock of make-up. She had applied herself to her lessons too, and taken care not to say anything which might give Reilof cause to think that she wasn't perfectly content and happy with her life, and although he still spent most of his evenings in his study and avoided being alone with her for any length of time, she told herself that she must persevere and not mind too much.

It was halfway through the following week, while she was sitting in the drawing room, working away at the petit-point she had always hankered after, when Piet came to tell her that there was a lady to see her. He spoke in Dutch to her nowadays, very slowly and simply, but she recognised it as a compliment of the highest order and she replied in that language, asking him to usher in the visitor. It would be Ella, perhaps, or Barones van Deille ter Appel, a formidable old lady who had known Reilof since he was a small boy and was embarrassingly inquisitive on occasion; she had taken a fancy to Laura and had a habit of calling at all odd hours. Laura put down her needlework and prepared to receive her visitor, but she was neither Ella nor the Barones.

Joyce stood in the doorway, looking lovelier than ever, dressed with an elegance which betokened money and plenty of it. She had, Laura considered, rather too much jewellery on her person, but she dismissed that thought as a spiteful one as she got up from her chair and went to meet her sister, thanking heaven silently that she was wearing the new blue denim dress, very simple, beautifully cut and obviously not off the peg. 'Joyce, my dear, what a surprise! We had no idea ...'

'I didn't mean you to—we've been spending a few days with Father and Larry said we could come for a quick visit, he's got business with someone at the

Hague anyway.' Joyce pecked Laura's cheek and sank into a chair and looked around her. 'Well, well, Laura, you haven't done so badly for yourself, have you? You could have knocked me down with a feather when Father told me—did you catch Reilof on the rebound? You live in style too—I had no idea it was like this. Reilof told me about it, but I didn't pay much attention, I imagined it to be some hideous Victorian villa. He must have a great deal of money.'

Laura didn't answer. 'Tell me all about yourself,' she begged, 'and Larry, of course. Have you a lovely home, and do you like America? You don't write often, you know, and then you don't say much ...'

'There's so much to do, I haven't time to write letters. I always hated it anyway, and we've three homes—two houses and an apartment. Larry is rich, you know, he gives me everything I want.' Joyce's blue eyes studied Laura's calm face. 'And Reilof? Does he hang you round with jewels and buy you more clothes than you can ever wear?'

Laura was saved the problem of answering this, for at that moment Reilof came in. He was early— hours early, and just for a moment she wondered if he had known about Joyce coming, and then dismissed the idea. She gripped the silver teapot with a hand which shook a little, and watched his face with anxious eyes. He had paused in the doorway, staring across the room at Joyce, who was smiling her lovely smile at him, but he wasn't smiling, his eyes narrowed for a moment and then his expression became bland, giving nothing of his feelings away.

After the tiniest pause, he said: 'Joyce...' and crossed the room towards her, but before he reached her she had jumped up to meet him halfway to throw her arms around his neck and kiss him. Not a sisterly kiss; Laura looked away because she couldn't bear to watch them.

'I'll get some fresh tea,' she said brightly to no one in particular, and clutching the teapot, went blindly out of the room. Reilof hadn't said a word to her—indeed, he hadn't appeared to have noticed her, and she fought back tears as she rushed across the hall to encounter Piet halfway. He took the teapot from her and said with gentle reproof: 'You should have rung, mevrouw,' and went off to the kitchen with it, leaving her with nothing to do but go back to the drawing room.

Joyce was back in her chair and Reilof was standing near her and they were laughing together; they looked round as she went in and he said easily: 'Larry and Joyce have asked us to dinner this evening, Laura. They're at the Hotel Hooge Vuursche—will eight o'clock suit you?'

Laura agreed pleasantly that it would and busied herself pouring the tea which Piet had brought in, aware that Joyce had taken the conversation into her own hands and had no intention of including her in it, although Reilof drew her into their talk whenever possible. And Joyce was at her best, wistful and gay by turns, grumbling prettily that Larry had to spend so much time away on business: 'All the way to the Hague,' she pouted at Reilof, 'and here's poor little me on my own ...'

'Could you not go with him?'

She made a charming face. 'And what should I do with myself while he's with his dreary business friends?' She smiled enchantingly at him. 'Reilof, couldn't you spare a day—two days, and take me out? It's such a pity not to see something of Holland while I'm here.'

He had gone to sit in his great winged chair by the window. 'My dear girl, I'm a working man.'

'Home at half-past three in the afternoon?' she interpolated quickly.

His eyes rested momentarily on Laura. 'That was for a special reason—besides, why shouldn't Larry take you? Surely he can spare a day?' He glanced again at Laura, sitting so quietly, her face a pleasant mask that felt as though it would crack any moment now. 'Laura has a car—I'm sure she would drive you around.'

Joyce's face clouded for a moment, and then broke into smiles. 'But it's you I want to go with, Reilof—there's so much to talk about.'

He got up and went over to Laura with his cup and saucer. 'We shall have this evening,' he reminded her, 'and now you must excuse me, I've a patient to see and a good deal of work to do. Until this evening, then.'

He smiled at her and then spoke to Laura. 'I'm expecting Jan. Will you tell Piet?' His dark eyes searched her face unsmilingly and she answered lightly,

'Of course—is he to go straight to your study?'

He nodded briefly, 'Please,' and was almost at the door when Joyce cried:

'Oh, Reilof, you must take me out tomorrow! I'm so lonely—and I thought ... I've been looking forward to spending a day with you, there's so much I want to explain ...' She had never looked prettier, but all he did was shake his head and laugh a little and go away without saying anything.

He had scarcely closed the door behind him when Joyce spoke. 'Well, you may have caught him, Laura, but I doubt if you'll keep him—for one thing, he's still in love with me, though I don't suppose you would know that—and you don't exactly sparkle, do you? He must find you dull ... Why on earth did you marry each other?' She didn't wait for an answer but went on: 'Oh, I've no doubt that he was in the mood to marry anyone when he discovered that he couldn't marry me.' She saw the telltale colour creep into Laura's cheeks and declared triumphantly, 'That's it, isn't it? Oh, don't bother to answer, I can see by your face—and you? I suppose you saw the chance to marry well and took it.' Her laugh was unkind. 'I can't say that I blame you; I'm quite sorry that I didn't marry him myself.' She looked round the beautiful room. 'All this, and some of it's priceless, I should imagine—but he didn't tell me, I thought it was just an ordinary house. He told me the furniture was old, but I never thought ... He's clever too, isn't he? Father was telling me—a professor of something or other and one of the best-known, too, with a marvellous future—probably he'll get a knighthood.'

'They don't give titles in Holland, at least not in the same way as they do in England.' Laura was aware as she spoke that it was a pointless remark to make; Joyce wasn't listening. She had curled her legs under her and sat, chin in hand, deep in plans which were nonsense but which somehow she managed to make horribly possible.

'Who knows,' she said thoughtfully, 'divorce is easy.' She smiled widely across at Laura. 'You may have him for a month or two, ducky, just while I divorce Larry, then all you'll have to do is to leave him, then he can divorce you—he'll see that you're provided for. You'll be able to live where you like. Yes, I think I should enjoy living here—it's got something ...'

Laura had listened to this amazing speech with growing horror and rage. 'You're mad,' she said slowly, 'and you don't mean a word of it—you're happily married to Larry.'

Joyce gave her a contemptuous look. 'Larry?' she shrugged. 'He's all right for the moment. And I'm not mad, Laura, didn't you see Reilof kiss me just now? Under your nose, though I daresay you're prissy enough to look the other way. He couldn't help himself.' She smiled. 'You never imagined that he'd look at you again if he could have me?'

Laura felt as though a leaden weight filled her

chest. It was like being in a hideous nightmare, only she wouldn't be able to wake up from it. True, she hadn't seen Reilof kiss Joyce, but then, just as her sister had said, she hadn't looked. With a great effort she kept her voice quiet and steady. 'No, I've never imagined that, but isn't this whole conversation getting a little ridiculous?'

Joyce got up and wandered across to the little walnut cabinet against the wall. 'You've always been a fool,' she observed. 'Do you really suppose that you can pretend that everything's just as you want it to be? I meant every word. You'll see, Reilof will take me out tomorrow because he wants to—then perhaps you'll believe me.'

Laura's voice was sharp. 'However much he wanted to do so, his work is more important to him than anything else. He would never neglect it for anything other than some emergency.'

'Pooh—there you go again; that's what you want to think.' Joyce opened the cabinet door and took out an exquisite soft paste Sèvres *trembleuse* cup and saucer. 'What's this pretty thing?'

Laura told her. By now she knew and loved everything in the old house; to give it up would break her heart for a second time. Not that she intended to give Reilof up without a fight; only if he really loved Joyce enough to go through all the dreary business of a divorce would she do that. She wanted him to be happy above everything else, and if to part from him was the answer then she would have to do it, but first she would have to be very sure that that was what he wanted.

'I must just go and speak to Piet,' she said. It was a respite; she gave him instructions about Jan, told him that they would be out for dinner and went back to the drawing room, pausing on the way through the hall to peer at herself in the great gilded mirror hanging there. The face which stared back at her looked exactly the same as usual; which considering that her heart was breaking and the little world which she had been building so precariously was in ruins around her, seemed extraordinary.

Joyce went presently, borne away by a taxi Laura had asked Piet to get for her. Her farewells were gay and lighthearted and Laura wondered if she had forgotten all the dreadful things she had said —perhaps she had been teasing. She went upstairs and spent half an hour deciding what to wear, and another hour bathing and doing her face and hair before getting into the pearl-grey chiffon dress she hadn't yet worn.

It had a high bodice and a low neckline, with long tight sleeves and tiny pearl buttons to fasten it. She put on the diamond and ruby earrings, added the ring Reilof had given her, and with a last look in the pier-glass, went downstairs. There was still an hour before they needed to leave for the hotel; she went to the little sitting room and sat in an upright armchair, spreading her gossamer skirts carefully round her before she picked up a book to read.

She didn't read of course, for a conglomeration of thoughts, all of them unhappy, chased themselves round and round her head. None of them were either sensible or constructive, and presently she discovered that she had given herself a headache. But she thrust this on one side, willing her brain to think lucidly. As far as she could see, she had two alternatives; to ignore the whole thing and continue to run Reilof's home, welcome his friends, arrange pleasant little dinner parties for them, accompany him to those same friends' houses, deal with all the petty interruptions which might threaten him or interfere with his work, and wave a cheerful good-bye when he went on a lecture tour. She viewed these tasks without much enthusiasm, but she had been engaged upon them since they had married and she was prepared to go on doing them for as long as he wanted her to—which might not be long, not if Joyce had her way.

And the alternative—to tell him that she loved him. An impossibility, and supposing—just supposing she was fool enough to do that, how would it help the situation? Not at all, as far as she could judge. She would force Reilof's hand and he would hate her for it, for whatever his feelings were for Joyce, he would consider himself in honour bound to remain her husband; he was that kind of a man. She would merely make all three of them unhappy. It would have to be the first course, at least it gave Reilof and Joyce the chance to be happy together if they loved each other so dearly. Larry might have something to say, of course, but she couldn't be bothered with him at the moment; she had enough on her own plate and he was a grown man, capable of charming Joyce away from Reilof in the first place. He couldn't be such a fool.

Reilof came in just then, and she sat up straighter than ever and smiled brightly at him. He looked elegant and remote and thoughtful, although he apologised for keeping her waiting. 'And that's a new dress, isn't it?' he remarked surprisingly. 'And very charming too, a splendid background for the earrings.'

It was a warm evening and Laura didn't need a wrap as she accompanied him out to the Rolls and got in, arranging her dress carefully once more, and during the short journey she made small talk about nothing much, pretending not to notice how brief and absent-minded his replies were.

The hotel was imposing, its wide drive and fountains clearly visible from the road, its elaborate towers and balconies looming behind them. It was a little sad, reflected Laura, that the first occasion upon which they were visiting it should be to dine with Joyce and Larry, for she remembered very clearly Reilof telling her about it, and adding at the same time that he would take her there when they were living in Holland.

But that had been when they had been on holiday in Dorset—they had been friends then. They had become friends again, or so she had begun to think, and now Joyce had appeared out of the blue to rekindle Reilof's love. Godfather had called it infatuation, but she didn't believe that any more. She got out of the car without looking at him and sailed into the hotel, her head high, and for all her ordinary little face and mousy hair, several people turned to look at her.

In bed, hours later, she reviewed the evening minute by minute. On the surface at least, it had been a delightful evening. Larry had turned out to be a youngish man, short and inclined to plumpness and wearing heavy glasses. That he was a man of substance was obvious from the diamond in his ring and the pearl studs in his shirt front, and as if these were not enough he made a point of telling them the value of his houses, the number of cars he owned and the many details of the steam yacht he used each autumn. Laura showed the appropriate interest, and listened to Reilof saying all the right things to Joyce while she studied her sister. She looked stunning in a blue dress the colour of her eyes; it showed off to advantage the diamonds she was wearing and made her hair more golden than ever. A man would have to be made of stone not to admire her; a reflection which hadn't helped at all because Reilof was flesh and blood like anyone else, and when she stole a look at him, it was to see his dark gaze riveted on Joyce.

The meal had been long and elaborate and Larry had fussed over the wine. He fussed over Joyce too, asking Laura's opinion of the diamond ring he had brought back with him from the Hague. He harped too much on his wealth, and yet she had the suspicion that Reilof had a good deal more money than Larry. She dismissed this as unimportant, for Reilof would have been just the same man without a cent in his pocket. For her at least. Inevitably her thoughts returned to him. He had behaved with his usual charm and courtesy, the perfect guest, ready with small talk, a good listener, attentive to Joyce and herself. There was no fault to find.

Laura punched her pillows into comfort for the tenth time. Whatever his feelings were for Joyce—and hadn't Joyce told her?—he had concealed them admirably. She slept at last, haunted by dreams in which he and Joyce wove their way through a series of improbable events, always leaving her desolate and alone, watching them from a distance.

But with the morning her common sense reasserted itself. Silly dreams weren't going to deter her from her usual calm manner; she went downstairs to breakfast, wished Reilof a cheerful good morning, commented suitably upon the weather, poured his coffee, gave Lucky and Hovis each a piece of toast and immersed herself in her post when she saw that the doctor was frowning over his own letters. But presently he laid them aside and remarked with the air of a man who felt inclined for a pleasant chat, 'A delightful evening, wasn't it? I've always liked that hotel. I thought Joyce was looking quite lovely—if it were possible one might say that marriage had improved her looks.'

Laura looked up from a letter from her father;

apparently her own marriage hadn't done much for her own appearance. 'Oh, yes—she did look super, didn't she? I'm so glad she's happy.' She paused, for it was delicate conversational ground; she wondered how he could bear to talk about Joyce at all.

His dark eyes rested on her thoughtfully. 'You believe that she's quite content? She gave me to understand that she had some regrets—Larry goes away a good deal, I believe, two or three days at a time . . .'

'So do you,' Laura reminded him with some asperity. She hadn't meant to say that, but the words had popped out before she could stop them, and it was an effort to meet his eyes across the table. He looked neither surprised nor angry, indeed there was the beginnings of a smile lifting the corner of his mouth.

'That's true,' he observed mildly, 'but hardly a fair comparison.' He gathered up his letters and got to his feet. 'I shall be at my consulting rooms for most of the day,' he told her. 'Will you be in for lunch?'

'Yes.' She tried hard not to sound too pleased.

'Good—I shall try and come home. I've a number of patients this afternoon, but I'll be home about teatime. Uncle Wim's coming to dinner, isn't he?'

'Yes, and Barones van Dielle te Appel.'

'Oh, lord, I'd forgotten.' He was on his way to the door when he turned back to stand beside her chair. 'Laura, are you happy?'

The question was as sudden as it was unexpected, and she could only gape at him. 'Happy?' she repeated stupidly. 'I—I ... yes, at least I ... yes, thank you, Reilof.' She was aware that it was a poor reply, anyone quicker-witted would have seized the opportunity ... but her wits were addled. She heard her voice, wooden and polite and quite unconvincing. He stood looking down at her, saying nothing, waiting for her to say something else, and when she didn't he said, 'Laura ...' thought better of it, and went out of the room, leaving her to sit there thinking of all the clever replies she could have made and hadn't.

Presently she got up and went along to the kitchen to discuss lunch with Truus—a salad, because Reilof liked them, and some of the little chicken patties which Truus made so well, and to follow a bowl of fruit—there were nectarines and peaches and grapes in the hothouse at the bottom of the garden, but she would have to go out and get pears and apples.

The little errand did her good; it was so normal to set out with her shopping basket over her arm, and drive herself into Baarn and practise her bad Dutch on the obliging tradespeople. It was a lovely morning too, and still early, and she didn't hurry. Her purchases made, she drove back home, wondering if she should telephone Joyce. She had said during dinner the previous evening that she might go with Larry after all, but Laura hadn't been too sure of that; she could have changed her mind—

they might go round the shops together and she could take Joyce back home for lunch. Would Reilof be pleased? she wondered. But wasn't that the modern civilised way of dealing with the situation?

She was still trying to decide what to do when she arrived back, and leaving the car at the door she let herself into the cool, dim hall. She was almost at the door leading to the kitchen when the telephone rang. She put down her basket, called to Piet that she would answer it, and went along to the sitting room.

It was Reilof, and although her heart had rushed into her throat at the sound of his voice she made herself answer his hullo calmly. But he didn't speak for several moments and she rushed into speech. 'Have you left something behind? Do you want me ...?'

He cut her short then, and said curtly, 'Something has turned up, Laura—I shan't be home for lunch, probably not for tea either. I'll do my best to get home for dinner.' He sounded hurried and preoccupied.

'What's happened? Where are you going?' she asked urgently.

'Not now, Laura.' He hung up and she replaced the receiver slowly.

'He could have said goodbye,' she muttered, fighting disappointment and a faint apprehension; surely he could have told her and set her mind at rest. She had been a fool not to ask from where he was telephoning. She frowned, remembering a background of voices while she talked. Not a hospital ward and not his consulting rooms—more like a hotel ...

She had been on her way out of the room, now she flew back to the telephone. When the clerk at the reception desk at the Hoog Vuursche Hotel answered she asked for her sister. There was no reply from her rooms, she was told, and who was calling?

'Her sister, Mevrouw van Meerum,' stated Laura, and added mendaciously: 'I was expecting her. I wondered why she hadn't arrived.'

The voice was eager to oblige. 'Her sister? In that case I can tell you, Mevrouw, that Mrs Eldridge went out about ten minutes ago.'

'Not by herself?' queried Laura, and waited with miserable certainty for the answer.

'You have no need to worry, *mevrouw*, she was fetched by Doctor van Meerum. I spoke to him myself.'

Laura drew a steadying breath. 'Oh, good,' she managed in a quite normal voice, 'they should be here at any moment. Thank you.'

She put the receiver back and went slowly upstairs, where she walked about, going from room to room in an aimless fashion and then wandering downstairs again. Presently, she told herself, she would be able to sit still and think sensibly, but in the meantime she couldn't stay still. She whistled to Lucky and Hovis, snoozing in their baskets, and went into the garden, where she would probably have stayed for the rest of the morning, mooning around, if Piet hadn't come to tell her that Jan de Mijhof had called and might he join her in the garden?

She hadn't seen Jan for some days, for she had been careful to avoid his company, something which she told herself was ridiculous. But Reilof had seemed strangely annoyed about her outing with Jan, and although she hadn't felt free to tell him her reasons for going she saw no reason in vexing him still further. But now she didn't think about that; here was a friend, someone with whom she could while away half an hour while she pulled herself together. She crossed the lawn to meet him, forgetful of her pinched, unhappy face, smiling her pleasure.

'Jan—how nice, now you can have coffee with me. I don't seem to have seen you for a few days.'

He took her hand and shook it, smiling at her although his kind eyes missed nothing of her wan looks. 'I'd love some coffee, although I really came to see if Reilof was here. His secretary told me that he has cancelled everything for today; she passed on some of his patients to me ... I thought he might be here, playing truant in your company.'

She shook her head and pinned a smile on to a mouth which shook a little despite her best efforts. 'He's not here. He telephoned a little while ago to say that he didn't expect to be home for lunch or tea ...'

'Gone off with a girl-friend,' said Jan laughingly, and stopped short at the look on her face. 'Sorry,' he said quickly, 'I make these silly jokes—I need a wife to make me toe the line.' He didn't look at her again but tucked an arm in hers and strolled back to the house. 'Actually, I hadn't intended to tell you yet, although you would have been the first to know for you were so kind and understanding. Ella has promised to marry me—on my terms.'

Laura stood still. 'How super—Jan, what splendid news! I am glad. I know you'll both be very happy, she's such a dear girl and so gay and pretty. When do you plan to marry?'

'Just as soon as it can be arranged.' They were in the little sitting room by now and she saw that Piet had already brought in the coffee tray. She busied herself pouring it, waving him to a chair opposite her own and handed him his cup.

He took it from her, hesitated and said diffidently: 'I haven't mentioned it before, Laura, but I had the idea that Reilof was annoyed because you went to Utrecht with me. He said nothing to me, but I hope he wasn't vexed with you? Did you tell him about Ella?' He smiled broadly at her. 'He would be amused that you should play the part of fairy godmother, I think.'

She ignored most of this and said lightly, 'You asked me to say nothing, so I didn't—it didn't matter in the least,' and as if she knew that wasn't quite enough explanation: 'He's been frightfully busy.'

168

Her companion gave her a quick glance. 'Yes. Yes, of course.' He set down his coffee cup. 'Ella and I would like you both to come out to dinner with us, but before that I should like to talk to Reilof about this house he offered me.' He stood up. 'You will forgive me if I go? I have quite a number of patients to visit after lunch and work to do first. I'll telephone Reilof later.'

Laura said all the right things, went with him to the door and watched him drive away; Jan was a dear and a good friend to them both, which made it impossible to confide in him and ask his advice, but at least she could tell Reilof now why she had gone to Utrecht ... She remembered suddenly that it really didn't matter now; what hope had she of improving their relationship now that Joyce had come dancing back into his life? She sighed, went to tell Truus that she wouldn't be in to lunch as the doctor was prevented from coming home, and with Lucky and Hovis at her heels, she set off for a walk in the woods.

The day crawled by and there was no message. By tea time she was both furiously angry and frightened too. That Reilof was spending the day with Joyce she had no doubt; had she not had proof of that from the hotel? But surely he would come back. Whatever his feelings towards her were, he would, for the time being at least, present an unruffled front to his friends and especially his guests that evening.

But it seemed she was wrong. She went up to

change her dress and returned to the drawing room to wait for him. Their guests had been bidden for eight o'clock; at five minutes to the hour she poured herself a glass of sherry, drank it very fast and went to warn Truus that they might have to start dinner without the doctor. And at eight o'clock exactly Uncle Wim and Barones van Dielle ter Appel arrived. Laura greeted them with composure, explained that Reilof had been detained and sent his excuses, and fortified by a second glass of sherry with her guests, made bright conversation until Piet came to tell her that dinner was served. They had reached the sweet and Laura was ready to drop from her efforts to keep the Barones suitably amused and her godfather from making awkward observations, when Reilof came in.

He was wearing the dark grey suit he had been wearing when he left the house that morning, and although he was immaculate as he always was, he looked preoccupied, but he greeted his guests with his usual charm and good manners, made his apologies for being late and dropped a brief kiss on her cheek before going to his own chair opposite her. He refused her offer to ask Truus to send up his dinner, saying that he had very little appetite and would eat whatever they were having. So she served him some of Truus's trifle which he hardly touched, and then suggested in her pleasant voice that they should all go to the drawing room for their coffee. But although she appeared composed now that Reilof was home again, she found that she was so angry with him that she could barely contain her rage. The moment their guests had gone, she would say her say, she promised herself as she embarked in her ramshackle Dutch on the recipe for trifle which the Barones had asked for.

At any other time she would have been delighted to receive such a signal honour from the fierce old lady, but now she didn't care in the least. She was all the more astonished, therefore, that the Barones should sweep her on one side as she was on the point of leaving and murmur, 'You are worried, child, although you conceal it well—one day you will be as good a hostess as I am, and that is saying a great deal. It is a pity that I do not know you well enough for you to confide in me; let us hope that by the time we are on such a friendly footing as that, there will be no need for you to wish to do so.'

She bent her stately head, and Laura, very surprised, kissed the elderly cheek.

Reilof shut the house door behind him and she stood irresolute, not sure whether to speak to him now or wait until he had gone to his study as he always did each evening. The urge to burst into speech was great, but she was sure that she would lose her temper and maybe shout at him, too. Piet and Truus were in the kitchen and weren't likely to hear, but one of the maids might come into the hall for some reason or other. She decided to compromise and ask him to go with her into the small sitting room, and was on the point of suggesting this when he said quietly: 'And what did you do with your day, Laura?'

She was so annoyed of being stymied at the last moment that she snapped, 'Nothing,' before she had stopped to think.

'Jan was here?' His voice had become very silky.

'Oh, yes—I quite forgot ...'

'How convenient. I had thought, although I had said nothing to you on the subject, that you had understood how I felt about you spending the day with Jan.'

Her voice spiralled. The entire household could have come into the hall as audience and she wouldn't have cared. 'Perhaps you would explain?'

'Certainly,' the silkiness was still there. 'You are my wife and as such I expect you to conform to certain standards. Jan is my junior partner and a friend of some years' standing, and he is also younger than yourself and he seems to find you attractive.' Laura watched his mouth curve downwards, as though he found this quite beyond his understanding. 'I have always considered you a sensible woman, but it seems as though you have allowed his admiration to go to your head. We are, I should remind you, recently married ...'

His words bit into her mind like acid into silk; she wanted to explain about Jan and Ella, but why should she if that was what he thought, and how dared he ... She said in a shaky voice, 'Don't be pompous! And where have you been all day, and who with?' She drew a difficult breath. 'I telephoned the hotel this morning—I wanted to speak to Joyce. They—they told me that she had gone out with you...' She gulped another breath, her anger nicely alight. 'And since you mention it, you don't seem above being attracted yourself, do you? Of all the nonsense ... talk about the pot calling the kettle black...!' She raised her voice and said very clearly: 'If I had a pot I'd throw it at you this very minute!' Having delivered this muddled speech she flung round and raced upstairs, banged her door shut and fell on to the bed. She never wanted to see Reilof again, she told herself, and after a good burst of tears, she spent the next hour wondering just what she would say to him when she saw him in the morning.

As it turned out, she need not have spent the best part of the night cudgelling her brain, for she fell asleep as it began to grow light and woke late. By the time she got down to breakfast, Reilof had gone, leaving a brief note for her; he would probably be away for several days, it told her; anything urgent was to be passed on to his secretary. He hoped that on his return they might have a talk, as there were several matters to be cleared up between them.

Laura read the brief message several times, trying to extract comfort from it, although she was finally forced to admit that it contained none. He could have told her he was going away, although on second thoughts it wasn't very likely that he would have done so, especially after her outburst. And where had he gone? She ignored her breakfast and flew to the telephone. The reception clerk at the hotel was polite and positive. Mrs Eldridge had not yet returned since she had left the hotel on the previous day; it was understood that she would be back to collect her luggage, as she had taken only a small case with her. Would Mevrouw care to leave a message?

Mevrouw declined the offer, replaced the receiver, drank a cup of black coffee, gave the dogs their toast and went up to her room. There seemed to be only one thing left to do. Joyce had got her own way once more, only much more quickly than Laura had expected. She wondered what her sister could have said to Reilof to cause him to turn his back on his well-ordered, busy life, his lovely home —he must love her to distraction. Laura, too sad for tears, opened her clothes closet.

She packed carefully, discarding anything she didn't absolutely need and taking only a small suitcase, then she changed into a blue shirtwaister and sensible shoes, put all her jewellery into the jewel box in the bow-fronted chest—even her engagement ring, although it hurt her to do so—and left with only her wedding ring, sat down to compose a letter to Reilof. It took a little time to write, for it had to be brief, sensible and friendly and giving no clue as to where she was going, only the address of her father's lawyer. 'So that you can contact me through him when your plans are made,' she wrote, 'and I hope that you will be very happy.'

She had cried over it a little and made a splodge, so that she had to write it all over again. As she put it into its envelope and sealed it down, it seemed to her that was what she had done with the brief chapter of her life with him—pushed it out of sight and closed it.

CHAPTER NINE

Truus and Piet would be having their coffee in the kitchen and the two girls and old Mevrouw Blok, who came in to do the washing and ironing, would be with them. Laura checked that she had her passport and enough money with her, picked up her case and went softly downstairs. She put her letter to Reilof on the desk in his study, left a note on the hall table telling Piet that she had taken the car and reminding him to feed Lucky and Hovis, and went to say goodbye to the dogs. That was the hardest thing she had to do, for Hovis whined softly and Lucky looked at her with his soft boot-button eyes, puzzled that he wasn't going with her.

She bade them return to their baskets, kissed their anxious faces and hugged them fondly before she went through the garden door and round the side of the house to the garage. The Fiat was cleaned and ready for the road, a job Piet did with pride. Laura slung her case on to the back seat and without looking back, drove out of the gate to join the stream of traffic going in the direction of Amsterdam.

She drove mechanically, not allowing herself to think about Reilof or the life she had left behind her. At Schiphol she left the car in the park and bought a ticket for the next flight to London. She didn't have long to wait, and once she was on board she didn't look out of the porthole to watch Holland slide away beneath her, but buried herself in the newspapers she had been provided with, reading the same few sentences over and over again without seeing them at all.

She still hadn't made up her mind where she would go when the plane landed at Heathrow. She was making her way rather aimlessly through the reception hall when she saw Joyce, looking elegant and cool and pleased with herself, and carrying a big dress box. Her sudden appearance crowned the personal nightmare Laura was in, and she stood still, not quite believing her own eyes. But Joyce had seen her too and came hurrying towards her. 'Laura,' she said breathlessly, 'what on earth are you doing here?' Her lovely eyes widened. 'Have you come to look for me? Is Larry worse?'

'Worse?' echoed Laura slowly, and Joyce said impatiently: 'Oh, surely Reilof told you—he had a coronary soon after he left the hotel the morning after our dinner party. He was in the car and had the sense to stop. What a piece of luck that Reilof was actually passing when it happened and stopped to see what was the matter! He saved his life, I suppose, for he took him to hospital and saw to everything and then came back to the hotel to fetch me.' She pouted. 'You can keep your Reilof, ordering me around, telling me what to do ... he's furious with me because I simply had to fly over this morning and fetch this simply gorgeous dress I'd ordered. What use am I at the hospital, anyway? And Larry looks awful, all tubes and bottles and nurses and doctors fussing round—I hate people being ill, I told Reilof so—he looked at me as though ...' She paused. 'He says Larry will get over it.'

Laura asked faintly, her mind at sixes and sevens, 'Did Reilof stay with him all day?'

'Yes—until the evening when he started to recover.' She looked curiously at Laura. 'But he must have told you ...?'

'We had guests and he had to leave very early today.'

Joyce wasn't very interested. 'I know—some doctor or other told me—Reilof was off to Antwerp to do something or other vital for some old man—not a penny to bless himself with, so I was told; Reilof won't make a penny out of it. I'd no idea he was like that—wrapped up in his profession.' Her pretty mouth sneered. 'I bet he comes home late and misses parties and forgets to bring you flowers. I'll stick to Larry.'

Laura said quietly: 'Yes, I think I should. That's your flight being called. I hope Larry is better soon ...'

Joyce had gone with a casual wave and Laura stood, jostled by the hurrying people around her. What a fool she had been, and now she had burnt her boats, Reilof wouldn't want her back; if he had loved her perhaps he would have come to look for her and taken her back home again, but he didn't love her. He didn't love Joyce either. Uncle Wim had been quite right, he had been infatuated and got over it like a child with the measles, and all he would want to do would be to forget her and go back to his busy, well-ordered life.

She wandered on to where the air terminal bus was waiting and got in, still thinking about him, not giving a thought as to where she would go. It was as she was getting out of the bus that she knew; she found a taxi and at Waterloo Station took a ticket to Wareham and went to join the queue for the next train.

The journey seemed endless and she was tired when the train stopped in the small station, but it was easy enough to get a taxi to take her to Corfe Castle. It was early evening by now with not much traffic about, and for the first time she wondered if there would be a room for her at the hotel, but her fears were unfounded; the holiday season was almost over and there were few guests, so she handed her case to the porter and for the first time since she had begun her journey, relaxed in the welcoming atmosphere of the old hotel. There was a room for her too, low-ceilinged and furnished with an enormous bed, an old-fashioned chest of drawers and a ponderous dressing table, but it was very clean and comfortable and there was a bathroom next door. She unpacked her few things and went down to the dining room for her dinner, conscious that she was hungry, for she had eaten nothing all day. Presently, nicely full and sleepy from the glass of wine she had had with her meal, she went up-stairs again; bed would be delightful, even if she didn't sleep.

But she did, for the first part of the night at least, to wake in the early hours and worry about the tangle she was in. It would be a simple matter to telephone Reilof, she reflected, but supposing he felt himself to be well rid of her, she had been stupid enough ... although any girl might have done the same. And he should have told her about Larry; all he had done had been to attack her about Jan—of all the nonsense ...

If she had seen him at breakfast perhaps he would have told her then, and she would have explained about Jan and Ella—it could have led to a better understanding between them at the very least. She tossed and turned in the wide bed, her thoughts get-ting more and more muddled. She had imagined, just once or twice, that he had begun to like her. She dropped off into a restless doze on the thought, and woke to the early morning sounds of the little town and thankfully got up and got dressed, her mind already busy once more. If Joyce saw Reilof, and surely she would, would she tell him that she had met her at Heathrow? Knowing Joyce, she thought it unlikely, and supposing Larry died after all, would Joyce turn to Reilof again? She had seemed disenchanted with him at the airport, but he was rich and successful and if he had loved her once he might well do so again.

Laura tied back her hair, suddenly impatient of

it, and went down to make a pretence of eating her breakfast.

She spent the morning wandering round the small shops and although she wasn't hungry, lunch whiled away an hour. She had been given the same table she and Reilof had shared, for the landlord had remembered her, forcing her to think up a tale about Reilof not being able to come at the last minute, and when she had sat long enough she climbed up to the castle, wandering about the steep slopes until it was long past tea time.

She felt calmer now, although she still could think what to do. She had money enough for a few weeks and she could always go home to her father, and surely she would hear before very long ... it all rather depended on poor Larry. She shut her mind off from the various possibilities of the situation and went back to the hotel to change her dress and eat her solitary dinner after having a drink with some of the guests staying there. They were pleasant and friendly and she shared a coffee tray with them afterwards, but when they invited her to make a fourth at bridge she declined on the excuse that she had letters to write and was a poor hand at the game, anyway. And indeed, she did have one letter—a rough draft of what she would write to her father's solicitor, but not yet—she must give Reilof time; she would send it in four or five days' time.

The letter composed to her liking, she brushed her hair and got into bed, and because she was really tired now, she slept at once and until morning.

The next day she hired a bicycle and went to the Blue Pool. The morning was fresh and the narrow roads almost empty and she enjoyed the exercise, and the moment she had parked her bike and saw the first glimpse of blue water below her, she knew that this was where she had wanted to come. There were very few people there, and she climbed the narrow paths to the place where she and Reilof had sat together, and perched herself on the rustic bench. The pool gleamed bluely beneath her, not a ripple on its smooth surface, the trees and shrubs already yellowing a little with the approach of summer's end. It was very quiet; someone had told her that the birds only sang on one side of the pool and where she was-there was nothing but the rustle of the trees as the wind stirred them.

The peace of it wrapped itself around Laura and gradually stilled her busy mind; it had been peaceful when she had been there with Reilof; he had enjoyed being there too, and she ... her head had been full of half-made plans and high hopes.

She sat on, oblivious of time, until hunger sent her down to the little tea-house for a pot of tea and toast before she cycled back to the hotel to eat her dinner with more appetite and go to bed early.

She went again the next day, not bothering to take a book with her, but just sitting and dreaming and thinking about Reilof and the lovely old house; she missed it all—the dogs, Piet and Truus, old Mijnheer de Wal, but she supposed that in a little while she would get over her longing to see them all again.

One more day, she told herself the following morning, and then she would pull herself together, write to the solicitor and make some sensible plans. It was almost a week now, at least she was used to the idea of being on her own again and had conquered a desire to burst into tears each time she thought of Reilof. She had no appetite for her breakfast; she made short work of it and set off for the Blue Pool once more, wearing the shirtwaister and a cardigan, both of which she was heartily sick of. Her hair she had tied back with a scarf and she hadn't bothered overmuch with make-up. She parked her bike and wandered round the now familiar paths, finding her way at last to the rustic seat above the pool. She sat there for a long time, lulled by the quiet, and presently she closed her eyes. She was on the edge of sleep when she heard footsteps on the rough path which led up from the water, but she didn't bother to open her eyes at once. When she did, Reilof was standing there, very close to her.

Laura sat staring at him, her heart pounding so hard that she had no breath to speak, and only when he sat down beside her did she make a small sound, half sob, half sigh. At least he was flesh and blood and not a ghost made from her longing; dressed with his usual elegance, too, although his face was weary and showed lines she had never noticed before. He took her hand in his and turned to look down at her. 'My darling girl ...' he said softly, and smiled, so that the weariness and lines disappeared completely.

She tugged at her fast-held hand and his grip became rocklike, although still gentle. 'You went away!' -she burst out furiously, but he took no notice, only picked up her hand and slipped the ruby ring back into its place above her wedding ring, and then kissed it so that she almost wailed, 'Oh, you'll have to explain ...'

He let her hand go then, and pulled her close and kissed her, and she, so suddenly transported from nightmare to dearest dream, kissed him back, so that Reilof kissed her again with most satisfying thoroughness. All the same, she said into his shoulder: 'I don't understand—at least, I'm not sure that I do. I met Joyce at Heathrow and she told me about Larry and that you'd saved his life ...' She thumped his great chest with a furious fist. 'Oh, why didn't you tell me ...?'

'My dear love, wait a minute—you met Joyce? But why didn't she tell me?'

'Then how did you know I was here?' demanded Laura.

'The car at Schiphol—no, let me begin at the beginning, my darling. I telephoned Piet and he told me that you had gone out hours earlier and hadn't come back—you had left him a note about the dogs, and he was worried, so I cancelled my lectures, went back home and found your note. I looked for you, my dear heart, I searched high and low. I telephoned your father and went to Uncle Wim and went to see Joyce, but she said nothing about seeing you. And then they telephoned about the car at Schiphol and I knew at last where you had gone. You see, I remembered the day we sat here together and what you said: That if ever you wanted to hide from anything or anyone, you would want to come here.'

Laura tilted her head, the better to look into his face. 'But why? I thought that you loved Joyce. And she—she told me that she intended to divorce Larry and marry you—that I could have you until she was ready ...'

His laugh was full of genuine amusement. 'She said that? But not to me, my darling Laura. Perhaps she knew when we met again that I hadn't even a flicker of interest in her any more. You see, I had been in love with you for quite some time, dear heart, although I didn't choose to admit it to myself and certainly not to you, for I didn't think that you loved me. Only on that day when I looked out of my consulting-room window and saw you driving past, looking so defiant and so small, did I admit it—I couldn't go after you fast enough, and when I saw the Fiat on the side of the motorway ... I could have boxed your ears, my little love.'

Laura said indignantly: 'You were beastly, and you were beastly about Jan, and I only went to persuade his girl-friend to marry him and live in your house, and you thought a whole load of rubbish—I could have thrown something at you!'

There was a gleam in his eye as he studied her face, taking so long about it that she cried quite crossly, 'Oh, don't look at me, I know I look a complete hag.'

He shook his head. 'No—you're the most beautiful girl in the world, and when I came home and found that Jan had been to see you I could have wrung your lovely neck.'

Laura sat up, the better to look at him once more. She might not be the most beautiful girl in the world, but she certainly felt as though she was. She said, a little breathless, 'Well, well—I never did! I thought you didn't care a button for me—I have no looks, you know, and not much conversation.'

'You are a stubborn girl, for I have just told you that you are beautiful and I find your conversation quite delightful.' Reilof tightened his hold a little and kissed her again, and presently she settled down against his shoulder once more.

'Oh, do you,' she asked, 'do you really? But there's a lot that's not quite clear.' After a moment she said, 'I think I'd like a cup of tea.'

He kissed the top of her head and said fiercely, 'You're too pale and thin, and it's my fault. You shall have all the tea you can drink, dear love, and tomorrow I'll take you home.'

She said a little shyly: 'I'm staying at the hotel.'

'Yes, I know. I called in on the way here. The manager remembered me; he was disappointed that we should be leaving in the morning. I told him that we should come again and bring the children.'

Laura jerked upright. 'Children? But we haven't any...'

'These things take time, my darling, but we mustn't disappoint the man, must we?'

'Lucky and Hovis will be marvellous ...' Suddenly she was crying. 'Oh, Reilof darling, I've been so homesick!'

His arms wrapped her close in the most comforting manner. 'Never again, dear love, I promise you.'

She sniffed. 'Oh, dear, I'm so happy, I think I'm going to cry ...'

Reilof put a finger under her chin and kissed her very gently. 'You may have ten minutes, dearest, before we go and have our tea,' and when she gave a little watery snort and said, 'I haven't got a hanky,' offered his.

She blew her red nose and mopped her eyes and asked, 'Do I look awful, Reilof?'

His dark eyes were tender, although he was laughing a little. 'Must I tell you again that you're the most beautiful girl in the world?'

Laura smiled from a tear-stained face. 'Yes, please, dear Reilof.'

Send coupon today for
FREE
Harlequin Presents Catalog

We'll send you by return mail a complete listing of all the wonderful Harlequin Presents novels still in stock.

Here's your chance to catch up on all the delightful reading you may have missed because the books are no longer available at your favorite booksellers.

Fill in this handy order form and mail it today.

Harlequin Reader Service
MPO Box 707,
Niagara Falls, N.Y. 14302

In Canada:
Stratford, Ontario
N5A 6W4

Please send me without obligation my FREE Harlequin Presents Catalog.

NAME _____
(please print)

ADDRESS _____

CITY _____

STATE/PROV. _____ ZIP/POSTAL CODE _____

OFFER EXPIRES DECEMBER 31, 1977   ROM 2110

Have you missed any of these best-selling Harlequin Romances?

By popular demand... to help complete your collection of Harlequin Romances

50 titles listed on the following pages...

Harlequin Reissues

Harlequin Reissues

Complete and mail this coupon today!